TAROKO GORGE

UNBRIDLED BOOKS

TAROKO GORGE

JACOB RITARI

Unbridled Books

Library of Congress Cataloging-in-Publication Data

Ritari, Jacob.
Taroko Gorge / Jacob Ritari.
p. cm.
ISBN 978-1-936071-65-4
1. Americans—Taiwan—Fiction.   2. Missing persons—Fiction.
3. Taiwan—Fiction.   I. Title.
PS3618.I755T37 2010
813'.6—dc22
2009053806

1   3   5   7   9   10   8   6   4   2

Book Design by SH ● CV

First Printing

The poem quoted on page 11 is "Song of the Master and Boatswain," by W. H. Auden.
The song quoted on pages 19–20 is "Sarabai," by Aki Hata, © 2002, Lantis.
The poem quoted on page 148 is "The Song of the Smoke," by Bertolt Brecht.

This dedication belongs to:

Tom Newhall
(without whom there would have been no idea),

Peter Piatetsky
(without whom there would have been no story),

and

Chris Castellani
(without whom there would have been no book).

C: Well, for practical purposes—but theoretically, that is only a partial explanation. An adequate explanation must ultimately be a total explanation, to which nothing further can be added.

R: Then I can only say that you're looking for something which can't be got, and which one ought not to expect to get.

· debate between Frederick C. Copleston
and Bertrand Russell ·

A man who goes on a trip has a story to tell.

· German Proverb ·

TAROKO GORGE

PETER NEILS

I was fourteen when I stopped believing in God. At the time it wasn't dramatic. I remember lying in the bedroom of that old, drafty house and thinking: If you *are* there, I hope you'll forgive me if I stop believing in you for a while, because right now I just don't see the reason. When you're fourteen, you don't have much reason to believe one way or the other. Everyone tells you what to do and anything you want is within arm's reach. Then you grow up, and you start disbelieving for other reasons.

But unbelief has its own comforts. You're not in such a hurry to figure everything out if you're not sure it will make a difference in the end, and you always figure if he *does* exist, and he's the forgiving guy everyone says he is, you can still make it in under the wire. And hey, the world's a big place, and there's plenty of time to find something you *can* believe in—maybe on the other side of the world.

Then you go to the other side of the world and maybe you don't find what you were expecting. You find something you'd just as soon not have seen. Then you come back and try to tell people about it, but you can't. When you finally have a story to tell, you can't tell it anymore because the person you were—along with the means you had for relating what you knew—is dead.

I should back up, though.

My name is Peter Neils—Nils originally, Scandinavian—I'm forty-six, and I'm a journalist. I've been in Nigeria and Sierra Leone, I got as close to Chechnya as they'd let me, and I was in the Gulf during the war, although by the time I got there most of the fun was over.

But that was when I was younger, still living down a bad marriage (high school sweethearts, seventeen, preggers, the whole nine yards—that's how it gets in Wisconsin), and I was probably hoping half the time I would die. As I got older I cooled off. These days I mostly do short pieces for *Vanity Fair* and *National Geographic*—pictures of waterfalls and tree frogs, the sort of thing people like. Nobody wants to see a hole full of severed arms. But for some reason people like to look at pictures of glaciers.

No one is ever frightened by a glacier—although, perhaps, they should be.

I was once profiled in *Esquire*. The lady interviewer asked me a question I assumed was just conversational, but it later—to my immense chagrin—cropped up in the interview.

"What do you think," she asked me, "should be the UN policy on intervention if the People's Republic of China were to invade Taiwan?"

You see there were no other political questions, so I was thrown for a loop, although it was a hot topic then with the hand-over of Hong Kong.

"If that were to happen," I told her, "I would personally en-list in the Taiwanese army and fight the Chinese. The UN can do what it likes, but Taiwan is a beautiful country full of lovely peo-ple, and I will die before I see those godless communists step one foot on its soil."

I had imbibed some vermouth.

That whole "godless" bit was a joke: I'm still more or less god-less myself (although I've flirted with the whole Buddhist thing, and my brother is very Catholic, which I respect). And it was more a sentiment than an expression of fact: if China were to invade I doubt the Taiwanese would be dumb enough to put up a fight, no matter how seriously they take their army. I just liked the idea, and I liked how it sounded, and there it was in print in a little red insert. My fifteen minutes, and I'd come off like an Internet wack job.

Not that I didn't get support. A lot of people felt the same, it turned out, but I'm not a radical by nature—I'm an observer—and besides, this isn't the Spanish Civil War; the days of Hem-ingway and heroics are over. Hemingway had a line about heroics being over, and how you die like a dog, but at least then you could still fight—even if it didn't mean anything. These days the gap in this world between the helpless and the heartless is wider than ever.

I'd first been in Taiwan—Formosa, the "Island of Treasures"—in '96. That was after the big chill when I got back from Russia and started looking and thinking hard about my life, and I spent six months there and six months in Japan. Japan was alright but it was Taiwan that really got to me.

The Taiwanese are good people. Maybe it's patrician and colonial, but you feel sort of protective. They have all the niceness of the Japanese, but more relaxed, more friendly, and without the vague doubt that their ancestors might have tortured your ancestors in POW camps (or, to be fair, that your ancestors dropped bombs on theirs).

In Taiwan, when you want to call someone over, you hold your hand out palm-*down* and waggle your fingers. That took some getting used to. Also, when you're a guest, after you and the host have put away some of that strong Chinese liquor, it's polite for him to sing a song for you, and vice versa. That was my favorite part. I got a kick out of listening to Taiwanese businessmen mangle the words of Beatles songs—which they assumed were what I liked as an American. I think a lot of people in Asia assume the Beatles *are* American. But my principal host, Mr. Lueng—a fellow journalist I'd met on assignment in Nepal—taught me a traditional ditty that goes something like this:

> *When someone punches me,*
> *I fall down;*
> *When someone spits at me,*
> *I turn my head;*
> *When someone yells at me,*
> *I don't get angry;*
> *It's less trouble for me*
> *And less trouble for them.*

That is a very—I don't want to say *Asian* sentiment unilaterally, but it fits a number of countries, not just Taiwan. Whereas it's not a very American sentiment.

I often find it going through my head when some nine-thousand-pound lady is hogging all the dryers at the Laundromat.

For years my life got quiet. I brought in a paycheck; I went out for drinks with old friends; I started seeing a woman, although it didn't work out. In '98 for *Vanity Fair* I landed a big interview with Rowan Williams, the Archbishop of Canterbury. I think they were right to send me and not Chris Hitchens. They liked the piece, and people—mostly religious people—wrote in to say my treatment of him and my questions were respectful. So for a short while I got a reputation as a religion guy, and in 2000 they sent me to do a piece in Taiwan on Fo Guang Shan.

Now, *Fo Guang Shan* means "Buddha's Light Mountain"; it was founded back in the '40s by a refugee who'd come over from the mainland. To hear them tell it, he'd built it with his bare hands out of nothing, and now it was the largest Buddhist organization in Taiwan with branch temples worldwide. It was in the Chan lineage, but as far as I can tell, all those places are like Protestant churches—more or less the same.

The order's founder was still alive but in Singapore, so I toured the main temple, spoke a little with the current abbot and a few of the venerables and some of the students at their college. It was a whole compound with an elementary and a high school. I say *compound* but I don't mean to make it sound cult-like. Everyone there was nice, and if there's one thing about Buddhism

I've observed: stated positively, you don't have to believe anything you don't want to. Stated negatively, you *can't* believe anything at all—if you're a foreigner they tell you what they think you want to hear, and I imagine it's the same for initiates. If you believe in God they'll call the Buddha-nature God. If you believe in science they won't mention rebirth, hungry ghosts, or the hells. There's a doctrine—*uppaya* in Sanskrit, *hoben* in Japanese—that's translated "skillful means," which says that truth can be expressed in any number of ways and *has* to be expressed in different ways to different people, and in Japan they have a saying: *uso mo hoben,* meaning *a lie is skillful means, too.*

That's kind of a pussy tactic, if you ask me, but at the same time you have to admire the balls on a theological doctrine that essentially says it's okay to lie. And maybe after all that's not such a bad thing when standing by your principles means strapping a bomb to yourself and blowing up the other guy.

I came there to report on the temple. I did the piece, and I turned it in, and I'll see if it gets used. I ended up reporting on something very different.

But first, something happened there that seems important now.

The temple didn't have a reception desk, only a big gaudy fountain-statue of Quan Yin Bodhisattva taming a dragon, and the venerable who was supposed to meet us had gotten his wires crossed, so—because it was a nice day and a beautiful temple—we started wandering. I was there with my cameraman, a young guy from California named Pickett, shaved head and a couple of bracelets on both arms. I had never worked with him before and I could tell he thought I was old-fashioned. Pickett fancied himself a Buddhist and had a mandala tattooed up his back that you could see on his neck.

Pickett was appalled by those giant Technicolor statues: "It's fucking Taiwanese Disneyland." I guess he expected they'd all be living in abject holy poverty, and I could have explained to him that that sort of thing doesn't bring in the acolytes. Was this skillful means, these statues, or was it skillful means to package Buddhism to Americans as some pragmatic philosophy? Did anyone know? Maybe the founder, but he wasn't telling.

"If the Buddha could see this shit he would cry," said Pickett.

Just to get him mad, I bought about fifty good-luck charms at the gift shop and hung them on my neck and my wrist, and I tried to hang them on his camera. He just looked away and muttered something about superstitious fucking bullshit.

The venerable we were looking for was a teacher at the college, so eventually—after a few bubble-teas at their café—we consulted a map and headed in that direction. The temple wasn't that large but as stupid Americans we got lost immediately. Instead we ended up inside the girls' high school.

The two girls we bumped into weren't shocked or shy at all; in fact, they thought we were teachers, and it took work—pointing at Pickett's camera—to get across that we were journalists. My Mandarin is frankly lousy, and Pickett's was nonexistent—we were counting on them to provide us with a translator—and while most Taiwanese take something like seven years of English, these girls were only so far along in their education. Next we managed to hash out the word "college," upon which they immediately and cheerfully agreed to take us there.

I wondered if they just wanted to cut class.

To be honest, I don't recall much what they looked like. But I think all Asian girls below a certain age are cute. Call me what you like, a racist or a pervert, but it's like I said: you feel sort of protective. I do remember one of them wore a white T-shirt that, when she turned her back to us, I saw read, *Drive away with me. Lot's run away together.*

Goddamn, I thought. But isn't that a beautiful sentiment?

As we walked past the athletic grounds, they waved to their friends on the basketball court and yelled something.

"'Do you like American men?'" Pickett whispered to me in spurious translation.

They took us by the back door of the college and one of them went inside, leaving the other alone with us, looking slightly nervous. We were standing next to a pool with big carp in it. Pointing at them, Pickett said, "Fish?"

The girl smiled and did a "swimming" thing with both hands. *"Yuu,"* she said.

Her friend came back with an elderly man who looked like a janitor. He scratched his head as he looked at us, and more slow communication followed. It was about that time our guide found us, running down a slope and waving his arms.

After that it went off without a hitch.

But it was later, sitting in a noodle shop outside the monastery gates with Pickett, that he said I looked "pissy." I hadn't noticed, but I gave it some thought and said, "You know, the more I think about it, the more I find that disturbing."

"Find what?"

"Those girls. How they just went along with us, no questions asked."

"You thought that was weird?"

"All I'm saying is, didn't their parents ever tell them not to go off somewhere with big, strange foreigners? I mean, *I* know we're both nice guys, but . . ."

"I dunno, man. It was like broad daylight."

"Still. In New York even the rich girls have more sense than that."

Pickett shrugged. "I don't really have any interest in fifteen-year-old girls."

For some reason I felt moved to respond quickly, "Well, me neither."

I can't remember what turn the conversation took after that—but we let the subject drop.

We had finished up by late evening and hopped the bus back to Kaohsiung. Taiwan is a small country, but it amazed me that a temple that was technically *in* Kaohsiung was still an hour's bus ride from the center of downtown. The one thing that has continually impressed me in every part of the world is the sheer *number* of people in it, the distances in between them.

This is an aside, but my brother Tom, the Catholic missionary, married a Chinese girl, and when her relatives came to visit us in Milwaukee they got out of his car, took a look around at what is by American standards a pretty big city, and remarked—looking quaintly pleased—that it was "just like the provinces" in China.

Kaohsiung is a sprawling commercial city, although nothing compared to cities on the mainland I've seen. There is no discernible rhyme or reason to it, and we walked from our hostel until we found a bar—it took all of two blocks—where we bought cheap, badly filtered Chinese cigarettes and cheap domestic beer. It is highly possible to get nice things in Taiwan, but I think we both wanted a sleazy experience in keeping with the smoggy and crowded Kaohsiung atmosphere. Every Taiwanese, his sister, and his cat owns a motorcycle. There were six motorcycles parked outside the bar—presumably because there's slightly more room than in China, where the bicycle is preferred.

We had two days to ourselves and we were pondering what to do with them. We'd gotten to like each other well enough that we planned to stick together. The sight of the temple had cured Pickett of his spiritual aspirations vis-à-vis Taiwan and now he wasn't sure about seeing more temples. There were some nice ones in the mountains, I told him. I had once waited for several hours outside a combined liquor store and poultry farm to hitch a ride on a flatbed truck to a mountain temple. He wasn't so sure about that, either, so I asked if he had ever seen Taroko Gorge. Of course he hadn't seen Taroko; it was his first time in Taiwan; but I was drunk. "You have to see Taroko," I said. "It's gorges." I think I stole that pun off a bumper sticker. Taroko Gorge is Taiwan's national park, closer to Taipei at the northern end of the island than to Kaohsiung in the south. It's four hours by bus from Kaohsiung, no longer than from New York to Boston. After we saw it, I told him, we could do the rounds in Taipei; I'd look up friends there and we'd have a grand old time. This struck both of us as a sound plan, although at that point buying two motor-cycles and driving them into the sea might have seemed like a sound plan.

After that Pickett struck up an acquaintance with a local girl who may or may not have been a prostitute. Now, I'm no pickup artist, wasn't even when I was young—residual Catholic guilt, I suppose—but it's not like I objected. She looked young (*no interest in fifteen-year-old girls?*), but let's be honest—who can tell? They went off somewhere, and I made my way unsteadily back to the hostel. I've picked up snatches of poetry in my time, and one of them came back to me then:

> *There Wealthy Meg, the Sailor's Friend,*
> *And Marion, cow-eyed,*
> *Opened their arms to me but I*
> *Refused to come inside;*
> *I was not looking for a cage*
> *In which to mope in my old age.*

I stayed up, getting sober and smoking off the balcony. I called a friend in New York and told him how the journalism had gone: for him it was almost noon. Pickett came back at past three in the morning looking drawn and confused. Although I was jocular about it, he wouldn't talk about what had happened. He had money the next day, so I figured at least he hadn't been robbed. I guessed it would always remain a mystery.

When it got light we hopped a cab to the station and got on the bus to Taroko.

My fondness for Taiwan might be due to the fact that my first vacation there was the first real vacation of my life. On assignment I had worked constantly—I had a real work ethic then—in the middle of grimy, noisy, sometimes dangerous situations, and I drank more heavily so that half the time I was all business, the other half nothing at all. Before that I had grown up in Milwaukee and New York, natureless cities of great industry. So I remember that first bus ride from Kaohsiung to Taroko Gorge. The road goes straight up the seaside cliffs, under arches of natural granite, and the bright blue Taiwanese sea is enough to kill the breath in you. The size of those cliffs is incredible and on a clear day there is no dividing line between the blue sea and blue sky and it looks like the mouth of God. And seven years later, it was just the way I remembered it.

To me, after that prelude, the gorge itself was somewhat of a letdown. But how could it have lived up to my expectations? The first time that ride along the edge of the sea felt like the antechamber to some other world. We just never got there.

Of course to my companion, of San Francisco, a gorgeous seaside drive was nothing new.

Pickett was surprisingly uninterested in my old war stories. He didn't ask about the time I had photographed a family of alleged drug dealers lying in their blood, shot at their breakfast table by the Nigerian police. In his presence I felt younger and probably acted it, so we talked about drugs, and the Doors, and Graham Greene. Pickett was a great reader and a graduate of Bard College. We joked that to find another drinker in the journalistic profession was no great providence, another reader more so.

He was newly enthusiastic about books I hardly remembered reading; also about ideas I knew to be ill-advised.

"One day, man, hell, maybe when this job's over, I'm'a go to Jamaica, smoke it up with the Rastas." Noticing the incredulous look I gave him, he quickly amended, "Look at you there, sittin' lookin' at me like I just listened to one Marley record. I got friends went there, they say the grass's so strong—"

"Damn right," I said. "It's so strong it fucking paralyzes you. That's when you say something dumb and it gives them the excuse to shoot you in the head."

"The hell you mean—? The Rastas ain't gonna shoot me. Whatever happened to One Love?"

"I don't know what happened to it. But they shoot tourists now, and that's a fact. Take it from me, I wouldn't go there without a very reliable local guide."

I'd heard as much, although it had been years since I'd smoked.

You started to see the signs for Taroko long before you got there. This heightened that unbearable anticipation I'd felt the first time, along with a directional sign that read—I swear to God—to the "promised land." I don't know if this referred to Taroko or to some other place. In any case the whole area was a bit strange. There kept being bigger and bigger cliffs, and you wondered, is this Taroko now . . . ?

But as I said, when you got there it was a letdown. The bus let us off nowhere in particular, by a rest stop, the other tourists wandered off, and Pickett looked around blinking.

"We here?"

I nodded. "We here."

"Big rocks," he said, as if to humor me.

We weren't yet in the gorge proper; there were still the mountains on either side of us. The gorge itself only substituted sheer rock for the foliage.

"Big rocks," I said.

He began to unpack his camera. "I bet I could get some good shots here. Maybe sell 'em someplace else . . ."

"Or just put them in with the piece. We can say we took them at the temple; they'll never know."

"Hah. Yeah. Dumb fucks."

"Dumb fuckin' fucks. Howie," that was my current editor, "thinks all East Asia is just one big jungle around a temple. And Tokyo."

We were both a bit vague with our hangovers, in the bright sunlight all of a sudden.

We lit up Double Lucky cigarettes from the bright red cartons. Double, lucky, and red, all the constituent elements of Chinese culture. It crossed my mind that the Chinese emphasis on luck was just about as far from Buddhism as you could get, even further than Christianity. At least they both had an element of providence. But there it went with the skillful means again.

Pickett touched his head. "Pete, I'm not so sure about this. This whole getting off the bus thing. You ever see *Apocalypse Now*? 'Stay on the bus, man'?"

"Walk," I said. "You can walk most of the gorge, and on the little trails the bus won't go down. It'll be good for you."

"Fuck, man. I ate all vegetarian yesterday, I dunno."

"I thought you ate all vegetarian every day. Fucking Buddhist hippie."

"I try," he said.

"You stay on the bus, they drive so close to the railing you swear the thing is going in the drink. It *leans*, man. Fifty feet straight down to the water. Railing a foot high, made out of tin. The Taiwanese are crazy; they don't care; they'll drive you anywhere. They'll take you anywhere in the back of their truck. They just say *Omitofo* and that's the end of it."

Omitofo was Amithaba, the Buddha of Infinite Light. He was popular in East Asia, so much so that he made Sakyamuni look like a chump. Reciting his name was supposed to protect you from snakebites, rockfalls, all kinds of things; another thing that had rubbed Pickett the wrong way at the monastery.

"It's true there ain't no seatbelts on those buses," he said. "I dunno."

"Walk. Take your pictures."

"I'll take my pictures."

His camera was old but good, a Nikkon F SLR. I'd seen those cameras before in places where they got dropped or even shot at. I guessed an uncle or something had passed it down to him.

We swung by the visitors' center, where I heard people speaking Korean and Japanese (both languages I had a better grasp of than Mandarin), and there was a big relief map of the gorge as high as your waist. Pickett whistled.

"To make it look good they show the whole mountain range," I said. "We'll just be down in this part here."

They also had a few stuffed specimens, all of them aged and a bit sad-looking, of local fauna.

"Damn," said Pickett, looking at a viper with seams showing in its open mouth, "I wanna see a snake. They don't have snakes where I'm from."

"Nor where I'm from."

"You think we'll see one?"

"I don't know if they have snakes. Squirrels they have. I mean the snakes are *out* there but they'll keep their distance. Don't fuck with them and they don't fuck with you."

"Shit, just like me," said Pickett. "That's my kind of animal."

Before we set off we bought a four-pack of Yuenling lager from the store, which Pickett carried in a huge plastic sack.

"Hey, man. You think you could make it all the way from one end of Taiwan to the other, just drunk all the way?"

"*Omitofo,*" I said, and we both laughed.

"Fuckin' *Omitofo.*"

As we went down the path, Pickett moving with wide, swinging steps as the lager bounced on his hip, he started to sing a song of his own invention to the tune—very, *very* roughly—of "Dixie":

> *Oh I wish I was in Taiwan*
> *It ain't China or Japan*
> *And they got big cheesy statues*
> *That they worship like they're idols—*
> *Oh I like to be in Taiwan*
> *I drink cheap beer all day long*
> *And something, something, da na na—*
>
> *Omitofo, Omitofo*
> *Omitofo, you motherfuckers*

I got this motherfucker with me
His name be Crazy Pete
I just made up the "Crazy" part
But he's pretty fuckin' crazy
That dude says he was in the Gulf
But I don't know 'bout that
Next he'll tell me he cut off Saddam's ass
And wore it like a hat. . . .

I joined in for the last chorus:

Omitofo! Omitofo!
Omitofo! You motherfu-u-uckers!

We got a few strange looks, and, guilty, I quieted down.

I'm getting to the important part. I should be careful.

It was a Tuesday, so the paths weren't too crowded. The last time it had been Sunday and the buses had been crawling down the roads. We took a footpath up through the jungle, behind a Korean family with two young boys, and the mother kept yelling at them not to touch anything. Halfway up the rise we both started wheezing because of the cigarettes and I doubled over.

"Stupid old man," said Pickett.

His mood was improving.

The bright, hot Taiwanese jungle. All of this so close by the road. Everything seemed painted in one pure color—green leaves, blue sky, red flowers. Birds calling. Some furry thing scuttled into the trees before I could get a good look at it.

"Nice weather," said Pickett.

"Isn't it?"

He set down the lagers and we each cracked one open. We sat on a rock that looked like Oreo ice cream and all of a sudden Pickett jumped up, shot lager across the path, and yelled.

Across from us, between two trees so far apart that it might have been levitating on its own power, was the biggest spider you had ever seen. Well, evidently the biggest spider Pickett had seen. Its body was black and yellow and it had legs as long as fingers.

I laughed into the mouth of my bottle. The spider was perfectly still.

"Man, I told you," already adopting so thoroughly his way of speaking. "Don't fuck with them and they won't fuck with you."

"Fuck, man," he said, wiping a stain on his jeans leg. "Scared the fucking shit out of me. Thing's big as my fucking head."

"He's just chilling out right there. He's cool." I raised my bottle to the spider. "I drink to you!"

"I fucking hate spiders."

"Hey, hippie, don't you think that was some dude in its previous life?"

"Fuck you, man. Maybe a real nasty-ass person. Like Jeff Dahmer."

He sat back down, his legs shaking a little. The spider was about five feet away from us.

"Have a drink."

"I will have a drink."

I love the way that alcohol and nicotine combine in your blood. When I drink I want to smoke, and when I smoke I want to drink, but I'm still alive. I lit another Double Lucky and so did Pickett.

For a second it seemed like I'd found that paradise after all—the one that was always just around the next bend. Always like that. There one second; the next, gone.

Kyoo-kyoo-kyoo, went the birds.

"So you love snakes," I said, "but you're terrified of spiders."

"Not *terrified*, I just hate the things.—When do we get to see this gorge, anyway?"

"When we get to the top we can look down on it. It's a long way down. The river should be shallow this time of year."

Then I heard them.

I want to put down the song they were singing. I know four languages pretty well—English, French, Russian, and Japanese— and I taught myself Japanese when I should have been learning another language, in southern Nepal, where it was the only educational book in that sad little dry goods store. It came in handy later. The chorus was all I remember hearing:

> *Tongara gatta sekkai*
> *Hikkuri kaeshi*
> *Hikkuri kaeta sekkai*
> *Hoppori dashi de*

Meaning: Turning the confused world upside down. Tossing away the upside-down world. Then:

> *Hai, sarabai!*
> *Hai, sarabai!*
> *Hai, sarabai!*

Now *sarabai*, as far as I can figure, is a strange pun. But then it was a strange song. *Saraba* is a slangy Japanese way of saying good-bye. *Bai* is just 'bye, as in *bye-bye*. I had never heard the word and at the time I didn't get it.

Three girls came into view holding hands and swinging their arms and skipping, as much as this configuration—and the narrow path—allowed.

Three young Japanese girls in sailor-suit uniforms. Blue-and-white jackets, blue skirts and red neck ribbons. My lager went down the wrong way and I choked, the colors were so sudden.

On instinct Pickett and I both moved our beers into less obvious positions. There we sat: two dimwitted foreigners, blinking in the sunlight. Against us they were brilliant and quick. Like fish, two of them darted behind the tallest one.

The tall girl covered her mouth and laughed. She had slightly wavy hair coming down on either side and framing her face, and a yellow hair band: this I remember clearly.

I swallowed a burp, a painful feeling, and said, *"Ossu,"* meaning, *Yo*.

Her face brightened. "Speak Japanese?"

"Un, chotto dake."

"A-aah umai deshou!"

Of the other two girls, one was sort of plump and had a bowl haircut; one was slender and had long hair.

Pickett punched my shoulder. "The hell you waiting for, man, introduce me to these fine ladies!"

But that phrase brought me back to earth. Feeling strange, I looked down and shook my head.

He put one hand on his chest. "Pickett!" he said.

"*Pikketto!*" the girl shot back at him, like she was spitting. Her cheeks were full of mirth.

"*Suman,*" I said, cutting my head at him. "*Kochira baka da.*"

I think Pickett guessed what that meant without my telling him because he punched me again. The girls laughed. It was bright on the path and their laughter was also bright.

"*Kiotsukero, kimi,*" I said. "*Hittori dakara.*"

"*Ee yo.*" She flapped one hand. "*Ee yo.*"

Although it wasn't exactly right, I had told her to be careful because she—they—were alone. She'd told me there was nothing to worry about.

Pickett raised his camera. "Smile, now! I'm a big photographer from *Time* magazine; I'll make you all famous!"

The other two were bolder now. All smiling, they threw their arms around each other's shoulders and flashed us V-signs. The camera snapped. All of a sudden one of the girls—the plump one—broke from the others and ran a ways up the path.

"*Taeko-chan matte!*" yelled the tall girl, then, as she passed us, flashed a last smile.

"*Sayonara,* Pikketto-*san!*" said the third girl and gasp-laughed and bowed.

"*Sarabai!*" the tall girl called back.

"*Hai, sa-ra-bai!*" came the voice of the one apparently called Taeko-*chan*.

"*Sarabai!*" said Pickett, waving vaguely, thrown by this suddenness. But he should have known that's how young girls are, darting from place to place like cats, like birds; like nothing so much as young human girls. Beautiful things flit through our lives like that. Other things, like Taroko Gorge, are just *there*.

"Cute," he finally said.

"Cute," I agreed.

"Man," he said, "real Japanese schoolgirls. Fuckin' A."

I arched an eyebrow. "I thought you said you didn't have any interest in fifteen-year-old girls."

"Well, no," he said quickly, "but I have friends who might."

I laughed.

"Hey—Crazy Pete. You got kids, man?"

"One. Boy." I pulled out the wallet and showed him the pictures. Steve. They were old pictures; Steve when he was ten, twelve years old, in the backyard.

Pickett laughed. "Motherfucker looks just like you. What's he up to now?"

"Dunno. I haven't seen him in years."

"Oh. Man, I'm sorry."

He stood up and hefted his belt.

"I gotta take a leak."

"Knock yourself out."

I took a pull on my lager.

"I'm sorry, man," he said. "That shit's heavy."

"Tell you what . . ." I shifted my back up against a tree, and my eyes wandered up to the speckled leaves overhead. "Take your time, why don't'cha. I might just doze off here."

"Shit. Well, don't get robbed."

I hadn't been serious—but while Pickett was gone, I must have fallen asleep. Here I'm not so clear on things. My head started aching a little when he asked about Steve. But that was no surprise; I had gotten next to no sleep the night before, and I was hungover and freshly—if only slightly—drunk. And I suppose it's normal not to be able to tell exactly when you fall asleep, let alone how long you sleep for. It could have been a minute or ten minutes.

All I know is that at some point Pickett came crashing back through the trees, wiping what I assumed was vomit off his chin. I was surprised he'd venture so far with that spider still hanging across from us.

"Sorry, man," he said, grinning. "Guess last night caught up with me."

Immediately I realized what had happened and looked at my watch, but I hadn't checked it before I'd dozed off. It was seven past three in the afternoon.

"God, we pissed the whole day away. Come on if you want to see the gorge. . . ."

So we climbed the hill, and we saw it. We stood on the rock looking down into that roaring pit. There was a wooden railing as high as your waist. The slope was gradual, but at that height it was still frightening. A sheer drop on the other side, just a wash of white stone as tall as most New York skyscrapers.

An elderly Taiwanese man came up beside us. Pickett and I

turned away. We hadn't seen the Japanese girls but the path had branched a few times.

"Should we just go back?" he said.

Maybe it was the light behind him now, but his face looked hard.

"Hey, man. You okay?"

"I dunno." He shook his head. "Still feel kinda sick, honest."

I imagined what, then, it must have been like for him to look down into the gorge, and I felt a chill myself. "Sorry."

"It's cool, it's cool." Then he laughed and said, "Big rocks. Whoo."

"Big rocks."

As we went back down into the shade of the trees, away from the sound of the water, he recovered a little. He began to talk easily, if unhappily. "I dunno, man. I don't think it's the booze, man; I think I got that out of me. It's just being *here*, y'know, out of the States. I guess it's caught up with me. I been away before and it's always the same. And those fuckin' statues . . ."

"Just homesick, huh?"

"Something like that, I guess." Then he added with sudden warmth, "Hey, thanks, man. You're a good guy, y'know?"

We heard a cry far off. Sharp but still indistinct.

I don't know why, it wasn't that unusual, but maybe just because of the awkwardness that follows when one man expresses affection for another, I tilted my head to listen, and so did Pickett.

The cries were coming closer. They didn't sound quite like a distressed person. There were several voices.

I tapped Pickett's arm and we started down, him with two bottles of Yuenling still in the sack.

I made out "Kari-*chan, doko?*"—a girl's voice.

Kari, where are you?

Then a boy: "*Oi,* Mori! *Joudan janee yo!*"

Mori, this no joke.

The girl again: "*Onegai, onegaishimasu!*"

Please, oh, please.

Then, although I should have known already, came what stopped my heart: "Taeko-*chan, onegai!*"

There was pain in that voice.

I jumped—but it was only Pickett's hand on my arm.

A moment later the boy appeared in front of us, wearing a school coat, scratching his head. He looked big for his age. He took us in unsurprised and said in fair enough English, "Excuse me. Have you seen three girls?"

Pickett and I exchanged a look. We had to admit we had. And then the whole business started.

MICHIKO KAMAKIRI

he first time I got caught lying, I was in third grade and I took a pair of scissors and cut the heads off all my mother's sunflowers. I think it just got on my nerves: Where did they get off looking so *happy*? But I told her I saw our neighbor Mrs. Nomura doing it because there was always a war over who had the nicer yard. Well, the war got a whole lot worse, and they were yelling at each other all day. Finally I felt so bad I started crying and told my mother everything, but I couldn't tell her why I did it. I know why I lied—because I couldn't tell her why I did it. She slapped me and told me I wasn't a human being. Then later she felt bad and let me eat some roll cake.

Okay. Here goes.

I didn't want to go on the stupid trip anyway. To make matters worse, they stuck me on the bus next to that creepy Bug. I was lucky, though, because I didn't have to be the one to ask if we could change seats: Chizu Sato asked first. But *she'd* gotten the seat next to Seiji Sumiregawa, and everyone thought she was crazy because everyone knew Seiji-*kun* was a total hunk—one of the top three in class A—but *I* knew she was just using reverse psychology because she liked him but wanted him to know that she didn't want him to know that she liked him. Someday I'm going to write the psy-ops book for junior high girls because God knows, just telling someone you like them, you might as well be committing suicide.

No, said Mr. Tanaka. No changing seats. Make a new friend.

Mr. Tanaka is *such* a loser. Who's actually named Tanaka? You never hear about any Americans named John Smith.

What did he mean, make a new friend? It was the stupid senior trip. In a month we'd all graduate and go to high school. If we were going to make friends, we'd already made them. And nobody, at least no girl, was ever going to be friends with Bug.

I guess his name was Keiichi Hirata, but he collected bugs and he looked like a giant bug himself: so, Bug. It started back in sixth grade, when we each had to collect twenty of them for the science project. Twenty was too many for stupid downtown Morioka, but Ms. Kazan was a mean old slave driver. All you got were cicadas, cockroaches, and a few weird flies—no spiders because spiders *aren't* bugs, but that didn't stop a few kids from bringing them anyway. If you brought eighteen, that was an A-minus; fifteen was a C; and so on. If you brought ten or less you failed. But Bug brought in nine, and the one he was most proud of he kept in a little paper bag so no one could see. Taeko Maeda, that *happy* girl, begged him and begged him until he finally showed her. But he *would* show Taeko-*chan* because even then he liked her. He probably kept it in that bag just so she would beg him to show her, since she sat next to him. But when she saw it she started crying. I'm not kidding: real, superbig tears.

Everyone crowded over: Taeko-*chan doushita no?*

It was a rhino beetle as long as your finger, glossy, like a stone. There was a green pin stuck in it where the wings met the body.

Taeko kept crying and asking him how he could kill something so beautiful.

You'd think that squirt would've learned his lesson that bug collecting wasn't something that made girls like you, but it got worse. I only know because he brought his box into class sometimes and the teacher would yell at him. Okay, I admit it was sort of interesting, and I'd take a peek over his shoulder. He had moths in there, beetles in all kinds of colors like designer stuff, spiders as big as your face.

Okay, I didn't *hate* him. Maybe I even liked him better than other girls did. I mean, I don't think bugs are gross or anything, although I don't like the idea of sticking a pin through one any more than Taeko did. It's just that this was the *senior trip* and this was the last chance to do a love confession before we'd all go to high school and work ourselves to death—on a senior trip the success rate for love confession has got to be like 95 percent—and that bus ride was something *precious*, you understand; it was a whole two hours you could spend with anyone . . . getting to know them.

Tohru Maruyama, the Class Rep. Rank: A-plus.

Tall, handsome, kind. The perfect gentleman. Maybe *too* perfect a gentleman. I don't think he'd ever even been on a date because we all would have known. Probably the kind of guy who would never figure out when *no* meant *yes*. In the final analysis a big No Way. There were at least six girls after him, and I'd have to take my place in line, and besides, everyone knew he liked that weird witch-girl, Kari Hiraoka.

Jin Sul-Kim: the Korean athlete. Rank: A-minus.

He'd transferred in in the ninth grade. There's a lot of prejudice against Koreans and I don't think it's right, but no one was prejudiced against Jin-*kun*. He had more muscles than he knew what do to with; first in track and a soccer player, and not stupid, either. Not as nice as Class Rep but not exactly mean, just kind of standoffish. The kind of thing some girls like. But stupid Cow-Boobs Sakura was going for the push with her stupid *breasts*—where did she get those; I think she must be Hawaiian—and *she'd* landed the seat next to Jin-*kun* on the bus from the airport to the hotel in Taipei, so she'd pulled a huge tactical lead. I think in such cases a strategic retreat is called for.

Seiji Sumiregawa: brains and a ponytail. Rank: B-plus.

They didn't like long hair at the school, and if Sumiregawa hadn't been the top male student in class A, I doubt he could have gotten away with it. He wasn't much in the rest of the looks department—his chin was too small—but the ponytail turned girls' knees to jelly. Also he told jokes and seemed experienced (although I don't think he *was* exactly, if you know what I mean).

Outside the top three, the prospects weren't good. There were a lot of losers in our class, and a lot more cool girls than guys, which was, tactically speaking, Bad News.

Michiko Kamakiri: the nondescript. Rank: C-plus.

No matter how much I eat, I'm skinny as a pencil. I guess some girls would kill for that, but I'm turning sixteen in two months and I want a stupid figure already. My grades are average and all I can do is play the stupid clarinet. You see? I'm honest. Maybe that's my good point. I do think my face is okay, though, and I'm tall, which means legs.

No question: it was Seiji Sumiregawa or bust. I'd push him down if I had to—there were still two days left—but I was stuck on the bus next to Bug with his huge glasses and his stubby little legs, and I didn't even want to go to Taiwan in the first place. Class A *always* goes to Taiwan, never Hawaii or Okinawa. There's nothing fun in Taiwan, no diving or coconuts or anything. All we'd done so far was go to some temple and some museum where the prize of the collection was a *cabbage* made out of jade. Just this cabbage sitting there. Mr. Tanaka said it was one of the great treasures of Chinese art, but I think he was making fun of us. What are we, stupid?

The senior trip: the oh-so-brief mating season of the junior high class. Like those flies that only live for one day.

Bug was playing his Game Boy. He'd gotten the window seat. I was leaning over the back of my seat, ignoring him, talking to Mai Mori, who was sitting next to Taeko.

Mai-*chan* was *boh*—spacey—but nice. She was no competition: like they say, nice girls finish last. Mai-*chan* was short, had long hair and big eyes.

Taeko was in her own little world, too, listening to music and nodding her head. She looked just like a kitten. Girls like that will make great wives someday, but it's girls like me who seize the day while we're young. We were talking—me, Mai, and (ugh) Cow-Boobs Sakura, who was behind her in the very last seat of the bus, about boys we liked, but not any who happened to be in earshot, which included of course Jin-*kun* and (oh God why) the Class Rep, sitting chatting with Magical Girl Kari.

Sakura, pushing her boobs in Mai-*chan*'s face as she leaned over her, asked, "Hey-hey, who do *you* like?"

Mai looked back at her with those spaceship eyes. "Like?"

"Yeah, like!"

"Like, how?"

Sakura cupped her mouth and whispered, *"Rabu-rabu."*

That *love-love* feeling. I sort of wondered when the language we used had come into being. So much of it was English, what had they called it before the English?

"Oh," said Mai, "I like everyone."

"Minna?" Sakura laughed. "It's fine to like everyone, but you can't feel *rabu-rabu* about everyone!"

"Why not?"

"Rabu-rabu is . . ." Sakura brushed her chin with one finger, "a special connection between two people . . ."

"Oh, I want a special connection with everyone, though."

"But special is *special!*"

Sure, Cow-Boobs, you should talk about boys, when they never leave you alone.

"I want to know if we're ever gonna see this stupid gorge," I said. "I can't believe we're driving two hours just to look at some hole in the ground."

Of course, if I was sitting six rows up where Chizu Sato was sitting now, next to the ponytail, the bus ride wouldn't have been a minute too long.

"I wanna see the gorge," said Mai. "I like lookin' at big things; it makes me feel small."

The thing about Mai was, too, she came from out in the country—rice farmers—and she had this real hick accent.

"You *like* that?" I said.

I hated it.

I tugged on one of Taeko's earbuds. "Hey, Maeda. What're you listening to?"

"Oh—hi, Michi! Did you want something?"

"I said what're you listening to?"

All of a sudden I looked around and my blood froze. Standing there, with his pop-star looks: Class Rep Tohru Maruyama. It was like a mirage.

He scratched his neck. "Eh . . . Kamakiri."

"Y-yes?"

God had answered my prayers! He was out there after all! All those nights I'd knelt down and begged for breasts and hips—not caring if it was the Christian God or the Jewish God or the Buddha; I'd strike my bargains with whoever would hear me, thanks—he'd done one better! Go on, laugh at me. Everyone laugh.

"Mr. Tanaka says stay in your seat while the bus is driving," he said. "Sorry."

"Oh." I put on my best smile. "*Ha-a-ai*, Class Rep–*san*!"

He slouched gorgeously away. I fell back in my seat.

Sakura was giggling.

"Shut up," I muttered, scrunched down, and crossed my arms. Bug's Game Boy was beeping. Up at the front, Seiji-*kun* was probably saying to Chizu, "Oh, you like blah-blah-blah?—so do *I*!"

"We should be getting close."

I looked around crazily. It took a minute to realize it was Bug who'd said it, without even looking up from his Game Boy.

"Oh," I said. "Thanks."

I guess . . . I felt like if I could get a nice boyfriend, all the things about me would kind of—snap into place. My face and my hair and the clarinet. All of a sudden they'd *mean* something—to him. He'd tell me things about myself I'd never known.

But . . . at the gorge Mr. Tanaka couldn't keep an eye on everyone. We might spread out. Have some time to ourselves . . .

Chansu!

But they didn't let us off the bus. It kept driving right through the gorge, so close to the railing that I was sure it was going right over the side. Taeko curled up in her seat and shut her eyes while Sakura pressed herself to the windows on the other side, going, *"Wah sugo-o-oi!"* Mai leaning over her shoulder, her eyes all bugged out.

Tohru came back again to beg us all to sit down. He was too softhearted to be a good Class Rep. I wondered what he and Kari were talking about up there—maybe she was busy converting him to her crazy religion. *Bingo*, that was it. Leave it to a girl like Kari to waste a golden chance like this.

Okay, I didn't really *hate* Kari; she was just *so* weird. And the weirdest thing was that everyone loved her. It's funny because her full name was Hikari, which means "light," and that totally crazy New Religion she belonged to was called *Mahikari*, which means like "absolute light." I don't know if her parents belonged to it and named her that on purpose. Mahikari is the weirdest religion ever. Going to church, praying, I can understand that (and for a second I thought it had really paid off), but in Mahikari they do this thing called *okiyome*. You're not even going to believe this if I tell you. They hold up their *hands* like they're saying hello and healing magic rays are supposed to come out of their hands. Okay, all religions have weird stuff, but the people in them—people who were in Ms. Kazan's stupid *science* class—don't really believe that, right? But Kari believed it. She would give you *okiyome* if you asked her. She'd just smile and hold her hand over you. It might have been more convincing, I don't know, if she'd actually *touched* you.

And of course sometimes it worked. That's just the law of averages, right? One time the projector broke in Mr. Okada's class and Kari walked right up and did *okiyome* on the projector. It started working again a minute later. Everyone was like, *sugee na!* and *sassuga* Kari-*chan!* When someone got a scratched knee they'd put their foot on a chair and have Kari do *okiyome* on it. They didn't believe in it but they didn't *not* believe in it. How stupid is that?

But maybe God—or *Su-God*, as she called him—did love Kari. Things certainly went better for her than they did for me. She wore a yellow band in her hair that had been blessed by the priest or guru or whatever of her temple or church or whatever. God, it drives me crazy.

And all of that would have been okay if she had just been a weird, dumpy girl. But she had the nerve to be tall and pretty.

Anyway, like I said, I don't like big places: I don't like feeling small. The gorge *was* pretty big, bigger than any street in Morioka.

I could see it plenty without getting up. I just wondered when they were going to let us off the bus, and finally they did.

We crossed a bridge over the river and stopped in front of a Buddhist temple. Outside it was hot and dusty and too bright. Mr. Tanaka was standing with Tohru and the driver at the front of the bus. The driver was smoking a cigarette. People in Taiwan smoke a lot. We had all started to run and laugh and horse around, and Tohru, with an expression like Jesus on the cross, started walking toward us.

People were leaning over the edge of the bridge: *Amazing! Wow! Too much!*

I couldn't decide which I thought was more ridiculous, this great big canyon—way *too* big for anyone to have a use for—or that little piece of jade, carved like a cabbage, that we'd seen in the museum. I guess all they had in common was being *things*. Maybe I just don't like *things*.

The temple had a gift shop, like they all do, and a collection box, like they all do. I saw a boy named Takeda drop in a coin and pray. I went over, dug a ten-yen coin out of my pocket—what did Buddha care? I thought—chucked it in, and put my hands together.

Dear Buddha, please let me have a good time today.

It was kind of a milder prayer than the one I'd been forming in my head.

I looked over, and Mr. Tanaka was sitting on a railing smoking with the bus driver. He was sort of smiling.

I went into the main hall. It was just a square building like the school cafeteria. There was a gold statue of the Buddha, and on either side of him scary-looking Chinese guys with swords, and one of them had a red face. I'm pretty sure I don't remember that part from when we studied Buddhism in the ninth grade. I went out again.

Taeko and some other girl were holding up little knickknacks at the gift shop like they were precious treasures and squealing over them.

I noticed something scary: the only one who looked as out of place, as squinty, as irritated to be there as me was . . . Keiichi "Bug" Hirata.

I started looking around for Sumiregawa. Points were scored when I saw Chizu with some of her friends at the soft-drink machines, and I went past them to where a little path went up the mountain. At the top of it was a funny tower, painted red, eight stories tall, and at the top of the tower, on the balcony leaning over, were three girls, including Ms. Big-Guns Sakura.

Jin-*kun* was standing at the bottom calling up (in his kind of broken Japanese), "Come down! Is dangerous!"

Sakura laughed and her boobs swung over the railing, like they might come loose and hit us. Feeling sick, I turned away— and there, right next to me, was Sumiregawa.

"Ever seen *Vertigo*?" he said.

There was no mistake. Ponytail was talking to me.

"I, I, I—"

Of course I hadn't seen *Vertigo*.

"Yes," I said.

He was squinting up at the tower. With his eyes closed like that he looked sort of amused, like a gentleman, like an English gentleman with a cane and a hat. I didn't care if his chin was too small. I melted.

"I went up in there," he said. "There's a big spiral staircase. You know."

"Oh, yeah, yeah." I nodded.

Then he laughed, so I laughed.

Chansu.

Sumiregawa was smart. What could I talk to him about that was smart? The only book I had practically ever read was *Musashi*.

"Sumiregawa-*san*. So—you like this place?"

"I'm not sure." He linked his hands behind his head. "I think all this—kitsch kind of represents a corruption of real Buddhism. Don't you?"

"Oh, yeah."

I didn't even know what *kitsch* meant.

Then he added, smiling, "Hey, call me Seiji-*kun*. We've been classmates what, three years?"

"Sure—Seiji-*kun*."

"Michiko-*san*—that okay?"

I nodded quickly.

"My friends just call me Michi. Or Mii-*chan*."

"Am I your friend?"

I smiled. "Sure, if you want to be."

"I think I'd like that," he said in his sleepy way.

Thank you! Thank you! The power of just ten yen! And maybe, I thought then in the bright light, *okiyome* worked, and didn't *everything* work . . . ?

"Three years," he said.

"And now it's all gonna be over," I said, proud of myself for actually saying something. "But I mean, we can still see each other—I don't mean you and *me*, I mean—everyone."

"I guess that's right."

Then a voice called, "Seiji-*kun!*"

It was like the sun went out. I turned around and saw Chizu at the corner of the main hall beckoning him. *Beckoning.*

"Ah. What's up, Sato?"

"Just come *here* already!"

"'Kay. Hey, catch you later, Mii-*chan.*"

"Catch you later," I said, standing and waving helplessly.

I stood there for a little while. All I could think of, to keep from dying, was that he'd still called *her* by her last name. Ha!

I didn't know what to make of it, or of anything else, so I started walking back to the bus.

But on the bridge I looked down and couldn't believe my eyes. There were *people* down there. And that wasn't all: *our* people. The Class Rep was down there! Tohru Maruyama was standing in the water with his pants rolled up to his ankles, hands in his pockets, like a model in an ad. And I could see Kari's stupid yellow hair band.

For another second magic seemed possible. It must have been thirty feet down to the river; there were no stairs or anything by the temple. Then I realized they had gotten down on the other side of the bridge, where the rocks sloped—and the world was boring again.

They saw me and started waving. I heard them calling my name. But they looked too happy down there. Kari with the light all in her hair. Stupid Magical Girl. It was like they were in heaven or something, and they wanted me to come, but I didn't want to go to heaven . . . it was too bright outside. I should have stayed on the bus.

But I went down anyway, clawing my way down the rocks. I almost lost a shoe. How could they all be so crazy—and the Class Rep? Kari must have gotten to him. That was just the thing she would do, climbing down a cliff onto a riverbank. I walked on the bank of white stone, and I could feel the heat through my socks. There were big rocks jutting into the river. Okay, it looked different here, like on some other world. Like the moon, only there was water—like there was life, all of a sudden, on the moon. It was cooler, too. They were all sitting or standing on a flat rock, right out in the river, and they had all taken off their shoes and most of them had taken off their socks.

It looked like heaven, but then it looked like some kind of Buddhist hell, a Hell for the Lazy. Mai Mori was lying on her back with her socks off, her bare feet just baking there in the sun. And Taeko was there, too (not Sakura, thank God), still with those stupid cute buds in her ears. They were both pretty good friends with Kari, so I guess it followed, but I couldn't trust *them* to keep an eye on her.

Then there was Koizumi, Class Rep's friend—maybe his best friend, you saw them together a lot—sitting like he was meditating with his eyes shut. Not that I had any time for Koizumi; he was a shrimp, even if he had a cute face. But with the way things were going, God, who knew . . .

"Michiko-*chan*, yo-ho!"

Kari waved at me. I climbed on the rock but I didn't take off my shoes.

"What're you all doing here?"

Tohru looked around. "Isn't it nice?"

"Class Rep!"

"It's fine," he said. "I'm here, right? I'm keeping an eye on you."

"Class Rep's keeping an eye on us," said Koizumi, opening one eye.

"Mr. Tanaka's gonna get so mad!"

I couldn't believe I was in this position. It's not like me, usually. But it just felt like something was wrong.

"If you don't like it," said Kari, nice as ever, "I was about to head back myself. You want to come with me?"

Taeko got up and yawned. "Oh, me, too. I'm so *tired*."

Don't do me any favors, I thought. I hate it when people put you in hock with them by doing something you never asked for.

Mai got up sort of suddenly and weirdly. But then everything was weird with her. She and Kari made a good pair. "I guess I'll mosey back, too," she said in that country way.

"Mai-*chan*?" said Kari.

"Yeah?"

"You were looking at that sky like you saw something you liked there."

"Oh." Mai smiled. "I reckon so."

So the four of us trouped back up the hill. All I wanted to be was somewhere getting acquainted with Seiji Sumiregawa. Still I felt like I had done something good by getting Kari away from Class Rep, even if I still didn't have a chance with him. When we reached the top I all of a sudden tapped her, and when she turned around said, "Hey, Hiraoka. Can you use your magic to give me some big jugs?"

It just slipped out. Taeko went bright red, and Mai giggled, but Kari just smiled.

Then she said, I swear to God, with a straight face, "You shouldn't use *okiyome* for things like that."

That was the last time I saw her. If I believe what they say, it might be the last time any of us saw her. Just when we were about to leave the temple, *Bug*—of all people—came huffing back, saying he couldn't find them. The rumors built for a while and we all stood there, and Mr. Tanaka stood there and smoked. For him I guess it was still a question of their wasting our time. Class Rep went to look, and about fifteen minutes later—we were all whispering so loudly it sounded like one person talking— he came back shaking his head.

"*Inai ka?*" said Mr. Tanaka.

"*Inain desu,*" said Tohru. "Hiraoka-*san*, Mori-*san*, and Maeda-*san*."

PETER NEILS

The first thing I did, strange to say, was call my brother Tom. The man was in Rio so it must have been three in the morning. I have never known that bastard not to answer the phone; it would give you the erroneous impression that he never did anything important.

"Hello?"

"Tommy."

My voice sounded hot and needy: probably a little drunk although I had long ago sobered up. It was five in the evening.

"Oh! Hello, Peter. It's good to hear from you. It's been a while, hasn't it?"

Only two weeks, but we were close. I'd called him when I'd gotten the assignment. He and his mission were building an elementary school in some godforsaken corner of Brazil, and God knew he had enough on his mind, but he would never say a word about it unless I asked. I always thought of him as a Jesuit, he was such an intellectual bastard, but the Jesuits have no lay order, and he belonged to the Third Order of Saint Dominic. The

Dominicans have had him running all over the world since he was twenty, doing just what I did, I suppose, except his wage came in the form of Treasures in Heaven.

"Tommy, I'm here in Taiwan. How's that for alliteration? Tom, I'm here in Taiwan at Taroko."

"How are you finding it?"

Tommy-boy was three years younger than me, but he had the soft voice of a child, or a much older man. If I had been thoroughly drunk he would have been too polite to make a point of it.

"To tell you the truth, ah—not so good."

"What's the matter?"

"I'm here at Taroko Gorge. Three schoolgirls just went missing."

I phrased it that way because it was how I thought of it—that simple fact. Without any context, Tom was politely silent until—when I was silent also—he finally said, "Missing?"

I realized it had sounded as if I'd been looking after the kids myself.

"That's right. There was a class of Japanese kids here. They just lost three of their number."

"Oh, dear. And they don't know anything?"

"Not a goddamn thing."

"When did this happen?"

"Over two hours ago. They're still here. They called the police, but I don't put much faith in the Taiwanese cops, to tell you the truth. I've heard stories. Maybe because it's foreigners, they'll get their act together."

"What do you think might have happened?"

A weird question. Had he guessed, with his Jesuitical sensitivity, that I was very much wondering what had happened? That it was, for me, still more a mystery than a tragedy?

"I have no idea," I said.

"I think you have some ideas."

Again that canniness.

"Well . . ."

The pay phone was in the basement of the visitors' center, in a back hallway. I was alone and it was bright and cool. Around the corner, in a room that I think was a cafeteria for the workers, were Pickett, a man named Tanaka, twenty-two Japanese schoolchildren, and a park official named Feng.

I lowered my voice. "A few rangers already combed the place around where they were last seen. They found three pairs of shoes and socks folded up inside the shoes. That's it. Tom, they probably just fell down a hole. This place is a sheet of granite sitting right on the water table. There are holes that go down a hundred feet into the water."

"But why would they have taken off their shoes?"

"They wanted to feel the dirt between their toes? Hell if I know. But there were no signs of foul play."

"And you don't suspect it?"

I sighed. "Who the hell cares what *I* do or don't suspect? Like I said, the hole theory seems most likely. And it depresses the shit out of me. Here everyone is sitting around thinking it's some big mystery, and in that mystery—I mean as long as there is a mystery, *they're still alive*—shit, I'm not making sense, am I? But there is no mystery really; right now they're lying in a few feet of water with broken necks. And the openings to those holes are small. You never see it—*they* didn't see it—and they'll never find the bodies."

"Wouldn't the park service," he said carefully, "if they had marked out trails, know about any natural hazards or such?"

"I don't know. The land's always changing—right? There are little earthquakes. Who knows what goes on out there; not the fucking park service. This place is huge. And anyway, they might have gone off the trail."

"You don't sound entirely convinced, that's all," he said with his goddamned Jesuit complacency.

"It's like that Occam's razor," I said.

"William of Ockham," said Tom, "was a strange man in many respects."

"Well, fuck me."

"Peter," he said, "they're lucky to have you there. You have a keen mind. Perhaps you are there for a reason."

"Oh, go straight to hell with your reason, Tom."

"You sound as if you're going to see this through."

"What do you mean?" I said, but then I knew what he meant.

"I mean, clearly this has affected you deeply."

"Maybe I will."

"Be sure to let your editor know you'll be staying. . . ."

"Goddamn, but I think I know my own business, Tom."

A pause and I said, "You are so full of shit, you and your reason. Fucking Papist."

"Just trying to be of service."

"Yeah." I sighed. "I know."

It was strange. Why should I be so shaken up? Somehow I had never seen a person die in front of me, but I had known plenty to go missing. Some of whom I missed very much. Nice people who had talked to me and then the next day were gone without explanation, in Russia, in Nigeria, in Sierra Leone.

"I'm getting soft," I said.

"They might still turn up unharmed. I gather it hasn't been very long."

"I don't know," I said. "I got a bad feeling. The whole thing seems *wrong*. Hey, listen. You've got a line to the Big Man. Say a mass or something for those poor girls."

"I will certainly do so."

"Catch you around, asshole. I'll call you up later and curse at you some more."

"Please, by all means keep me posted."

"You busy up there?"

"Never *too* busy, Peter."

"Thanks."

The click of the receiver sounded lonely.

A part of me didn't want to go back into the room. The only other Westerner there was Pickett, and for some reason I didn't feel as close a kinship with him as before.

When I was thirty I would have waded into a situation like this; you couldn't have held me back. I really was getting soft.

I went back in. There were three long tables in there, folding tables with round blue stools attached; two snack machines and a soft-drink machine; three fluorescent bars on the ceiling casting a too-dim light that made everything look grimy. The school-kids were all clustered at one table whispering together. Boys in their navy coats, girls in their white-and-blue blouses. Dark heads bent together. The next table was empty, and at the far one sat

Pickett and the man from the park service, two seats apart. Mr. Tanaka, the teacher, was leaning against the wall by the soft-drink machine, sipping one of our lagers. Pickett was nursing the other.

Three adult males. Pickett was rolling the lager bottle between his hands and staring into it. It was half empty. The top of his bald, sunburned head was the color of mud and his eyes were red.

The man from the parks, Feng, wore a tan uniform with a patch on the shoulder. He was older, wore glasses, and his hair was thinning. He held his head between his hands. I understood, of course, why he was distressed, but still I was surprised he would let it show.

Mr. Tanaka was young and swarthy in the way some Japanese are, stocky, with a lantern jaw and a crew cut. He looked up when I came in. I approached him and put out my hand and he shook with his left.

"Speak English?"

"Yes," he said. "Some."

That meant he was near-fluent.

"Hi, I'm Peter Neils."

He must have caught my name when I'd talked with Feng, but it was a situation where people have other things on their mind than the names of new acquaintances.

"The journalist."

"That's right, I'm a journalist."

"Reporter?"

"I'm more in the—freelance line of things. Freelance?"

"Investigating."

"Sort of. But I just happened to be here."

I dug a business card out of my wallet, and he took it with an apologetic smile, saying, "I haven't got mine. Tanaka Ryuhei—it's a pleasure to meet you."

That Japanese politeness that some people mistook for friendliness.

"Yoroshiku onegaishimasu."

He raised an eyebrow. *"Nihongo daijoubu?"*

"Iie, iie, chotto dake—Your English is very good."

"Thank you."

"I, ah, I'm sorry to bother you at a time like this, but I feel involved. My friend and I saw your girls."

"Ahh." The eyebrow stayed up. "When and where?"

"On a path not far from the entrance," I said, just like I'd told Feng. "Halfway up the mountain. I could show anyone the place. About the time, I don't know . . . but my friend took a picture of them. His camera should say what time the picture was taken."

"A picture!" Tanaka seemed heartened. "Tell me, how did they seem?"

"Happy. They seemed happy."

"It makes me very worried," said Tanaka. "Very sick. I was the homeroom teacher for this class three years. I know all of them."

"Yes, it must be terrible. But we still have every reason to hope. Do you know when the police are getting here?"

"Ask him." Tanaka cut his big chin at Feng.

"I don't know police," said Feng in much inferior English. "Very sorry. Very sorry."

"It's perfectly alright," I assured him. "No one can help these things."

"We bring out helicopter," he said. "Lots men. Lots dogs. Find girls in no time."

Lost men, it sounded like. *Lost dogs.*

"Do many people . . . go missing here?" I asked him.

I hadn't mean to be confrontational, but it was a poorly posed question.

"No one go missing! Park very safe! We work hard, all path safe! No one missing!"

"I'm sorry, I'm sorry, I was only curious. . . ."

Tanaka tapped his pocket. "I'm going to get a smoke. Do you smoke, Mr. Neils?"

"Is the pope Catholic? Sorry, American joke."

"I understand. Ha ha."

"Hey, Pickett, come with?"

He looked around at me with his bleary eyes. "You know what I need right now? A fucking *joint*, man. Mother*fuck* your cigarettes." But he got up anyway.

"Lots dogs," Feng was saying. "Lots men. No time, find."

I wasn't about to dispute with him in front of Tanaka. And what was he supposed to say? But I could imagine men and dogs crawling like ants all over the gorge, and I couldn't imagine them finding anything. Bodies in the river could wash up anywhere, miles away. Bodies in holes would sit there forever. And there were, of course, other possibilities that could not be considered but stood there anyway.

"Maruyama," said Tanaka.

A student looked up, white-faced. It was the tall boy who'd met us on the path.

"Take care of things here," he said in Japanese. "I'll be back."

"Wakarimashita."

The three of us climbed the stairs in silence. We came out in the room with the relief map, now dark and empty; I don't know if the park usually closed at that time or if they had closed it specially.

Tanaka stood with a pack of Peony cigarettes in his hand, looking down at the map. So it had struck him, too. Each tiny wrinkle of that map represented about a mile.

"'Very safe,'" he muttered with vitriol I had rarely encountered from a Japanese man.

"Your school has sent classes here in the past, correct?" I asked. "And you've never lost anyone—I mean, even briefly?"

He shook his head. "First time. Or, that is to say, boys and girls have been lost but always found within a half of an hour."

"It's not your fault," I said.

"I never should have let them get out of my sight. I was not supposed to. But," he shook his head, "it was a beautiful day."

"You can't hold yourself responsible for what happens."

"Yeah, man," said Pickett. "Shit happens. Fucking shit happens, man. Can't do nothing about it."

"I'm going to lose my job. I'll never be able to work again. I'll have to start going to some temple to pray for my soul."

We stepped outside. The sun was still bright and a few flies circled us. Pickett took out his steel Zippo and lit our cigarettes.

"I'm a physical education teacher," said Tanaka. "They never should have made me homeroom teacher. What do I know about looking after children? I don't even have children of my own."

"This is fucked up, man," said Pickett.

"I'm sorry, but I think both of you are overreacting. You heard what that guy Feng said. They'll do everything they can."

But why was I lying through my teeth? They felt it just like I did.

I went on lying: "Of course it's natural to react like this. When it's kids, girls, it just touches a nerve. But I'm sure when this is all worked out, we're going to feel silly. We'll feel silly we got so bent out of shape about it."

"So," said Tanaka, "tell me your explanation."

"Hmm?"

"Your explanation. Of how they could be safe."

It was a fair question. "Okay. They fell asleep. They didn't hear the men calling them. Pretty soon they'll wake up and wander back. Or they fell off a rock and knocked their heads. Unconscious. They'll wake up, come back; or if they can't find their way, the dogs and the men will find them tomorrow."

"What about snakes?" said Tanaka. "And spiders?"

"Snakes very rarely bite humans unprovoked. If the girls are out there, I think they would have the sense to stay put till tomorrow. And as for spiders, I don't know of any hunting spiders in this area—they mostly stay in the trees."

"Don't fuck with them, they don't fuck with you," said Pickett.

"Another possibility is that they're playing a prank on us."

"Hiraoka-*san* would never do that," said Tanaka firmly.

"Hiraoka. The tall girl?" Somehow I had guessed it.

"Yes. All three of them were good girls. The best girls. If Maruyama were not Class Representative, Hiraoka would be. She is a responsible girl. I can't believe she would do something like this. And Maeda and Mori were good girls, too."

"Alright, scratch that last theory."

Tanaka looked at me. Call me a racist, but it's the truth: I have always had extreme difficulty reading the facial expressions of Asian men.

"You are good at making theories, Mr. Neils."

I wasn't sure what to say to that. I smoked. Tanaka smoked and drank from his bottle. Pickett threw his empty bottle into the grass, and neither of us chided him.

"You ever been in Taiwan before?" I asked Tanaka.

"No. This is the first time I've been with students."

"Then you haven't dealt with the police?"

He shook his head.

"Well, if you need some help," I said, "a foreign journalist has a lot of clout in these situations."

"Thank you."

I didn't need to explain what *clout* meant.

"If they know I'm reporting on this, they'll make sure they look good."

He gave me a strange look. "Are you going to report?"

"I don't know," I said. "That depends. There might not be anything to report on."

Not long after that Tanaka stepped on his cigarette butt and went back inside, and I was alone with Pickett.

We stood on a hill. Across from us was the mountainside covered with trees: tiny, uniform trees. Now it was getting darker and they were no longer that bright, vivid green, more a greenish-gray. It made them look older. Birdcalls in the air. The sky turning red over the mountaintops.

"Pretty soon the mosquitoes'll come out like anything," I said.

"Well, shit."

He'd lit another cigarette. I just stood with my hands in my pockets.

"Crazy Pete," he said, "did you mean all that shit just now?"

"No."

"Not a word of it?"

"Not a single word."

"Not even about the snakes?"

"There are snakes and spiders that'll kill you dead in a second, I'm sure."

"Shit." He looked down at his scuffed boot toes. "They're gone, aren't they? I mean like *gone*."

"The police should be here any minute. It's been hours," I said. "They'll talk to us but they won't go looking while it's dark. They'll look in the morning. If they don't find those girls alive by the time it gets dark tomorrow, I think the best we can hope for is that they'll find the bodies."

"Well—don't fuckin' sugarcoat it, man."

"That's just my experience."

"Fuck."

"I would be thrilled to be wrong, believe me."

He put out his half-lit cigarette under his heel and turned to go back in.

"They'll want the camera as evidence," I said. "Where'd you put it?"

"In the river."

I turned to him. "Man, don't fuck with me. Come on."

"I'm not fucking kidding!" He brushed at his head like there were already mosquitoes. "I'm sorry, man. I went to take a shot but my hands were shaking so bad . . ."

"Why were you taking a shot?"

"Just to take my mind off—! Fuck, I mean, that's what I came for. Right? I just wanted me a nice shot of the river. Right out of my hands, man; right off the railing."

"You have got to be fucking shitting me."

"No!"

"You have seriously got to be—"

"I'm fucking sorry, man! Those girls—never hurt anyone. I mean they're just like the most *innocent*—I just wanted a picture. It's what I do. Take my mind off it."

"Pickett," I said. "You dumb shit."

"I know. It was a stupid thing to do."

"You stupid fucking shit."

"Fuck you, man. Back off. Back off, alright?"

I took a deep breath. "Okay."

God knows we don't think clearly all the time. He did look confused, and sad, and angry. Then his eyes met mine and it was getting dark, but they were bright.

"You don't think I did it *on purpose*—?"

"Hey, now! Why the fuck would I think that?"

"I don't know, man; why the fuck *would* you think that?"

"I don't know. You tell me why the fuck you thought I would think that."

He looked at me. And I looked back.

"Let's drop it," I said.

He looked away.

"You just tell the police what you told me. I understand. It's not that important. Like I said, it won't make any difference anyway."

"Who the fuck said anything about—" He shut his eyes. "Jesus."

"Come on," I said, putting my hand on his shoulder. "Let's go inside."

TOHRU MARUYAMA

know you're probably not going to believe me. I have visions.

I mean I have dreams: dreams that bad things are going to happen, dreams that good things are going to happen. Crazy, right? I know no one else would believe me. I'm the Class Representative, and the Class Representative isn't supposed to do crazy things like have visions, and that's why I never told anyone before.

When I was ten years old I had a dream about a snake. It wasn't even like a nightmare, but the next day my sister got really sick. She was in the hospital for three months with some flu from the continent. Then later I had a dream about goldenrod— you know, the plant—and a week later she got mostly better and they let her come home.

It doesn't happen a lot, and sometimes I forget about it. But when it happens I know it, and I don't tell anyone, and I get sort of scared.

I don't get scared because I know bad things are going to happen; I know they would happen anyway, and it's not like I always know right after the dream what's going to happen. I get scared because I start wondering if I am this way for a reason. My family isn't religious. We never go to a temple or a church or anything, except on New Years', so I don't know if this is a natural ability of mine or if it has something to do with spirits. Sometimes I read one of those magazines they put out about supernatural stuff, but I'm always like, what if someone sees me? Rumors spread like crazy.

I mean it's not like there weren't other things in my life. Most of the time I didn't even think about it; I was too busy with school and soccer and video games, and then with Class Rep stuff. I was born to be Class Rep. Ever since I can remember, I wanted to be someone people could count on—they'd be like, Oh, Tohru's here, things will be okay now. And then I wished they could look up to me *more*, that they could see how brave I was, like a general, if we really got in trouble. Then when *it* happened, I felt like it was my fault for having that stupid wish.

The night before the trip I had a dream of a tree that was on fire. There'd been some brushfires on the news the night before, and I thought that was probably why; then I started to wonder. I got scared that something was going to happen—like the plane going down. But then the plane landed and I felt a little better. Then I was scared that the bus was going to crash, but we got to the hotel and it didn't burn down, and we went to the museum and we were fine there. But when we got back on the bus, I couldn't stop thinking about that movie *Battle Royale*: you know, where they gas the kids on the bus and then they wake up on an island and have to kill each other. That movie scared the hell out of me when I saw it, so I guess it was just an old fear—and I didn't really think *that* was going to happen—but still. No matter how many things went right, I just couldn't shake the sense that something was going to go wrong.

I thought about telling Kari. She was in that New Religion, the Mahikari—just like her name—and I really thought she might understand. People say the New Religions are all crazy, but they also don't believe in things like visions, and Kari didn't *seem* crazy. She was just really smart and nice . . . and pretty.

It must be cool to be religious—to feel like all those weird things out there have something to *do* with you. But then, just to know the weird things *are* out there, and not know what they're like, or have any control over them at all.

The thing about Kari was she loved everyone, so it was hard to get alone with her. There were always people around her. And she took care of sick dogs and cats in her house . . . I mean, I don't want to make her sound like some kind of saint—I don't know if that healing thing she did really worked, except it made people *feel* better—she was just a nice girl. And it's hard, when someone is nice, to want them to be nicer to you than to everyone else.

I felt so lucky when I got the seat next to her on the bus. It was like a sign. But then I was so busy worrying about everyone else that I never actually got to talk to her. And when we did talk, it was just about the class—about how we were all friends, and we'd gotten so close, but in a couple of weeks we'd be saying good-bye, and that made us both sad. But Kari said something I remember: "Two people who've ever met can't *really* be apart."

When we went to high school, I wouldn't be Class Rep anymore. I would just be some underclassman. Kari wouldn't be the nicest girl in class anymore, and Otsuki Sakura wouldn't have the biggest breasts, and Jin Sul-Kim wouldn't be the only Korean or the fastest runner. But just sitting next to Kari calmed me down. I started thinking my being scared had to do with that, with it all being over. The bad thing that was going to happen on the trip was that it would be over, and then it was *all* over. Thinking that made me happy and sad at the same time. I could laugh and talk with everyone, and I decided that when we got to the temple we could relax a little, just have some free time, and when we got off the bus I could see Mr. Tanaka felt the same way. He was even smoking, which he never let himself do around us.

So I guess talking to her *did* do some good, even if I never told her about the dreams.

Or that was what I thought.

Then it happened, and I started to die. As of right now I really have no will to live in this world. That sounds like too much, but I can't think of any other way of saying it. It's not that I want to kill myself, I just want things to *end*. Like this was a dream and I wish I could wake up. Because after it happened, everything started being so much like a dream. . . .

But I couldn't tell them that. Because the Class Rep isn't supposed to do crazy things like hurting so much inside he wishes he were dead.

We were all sitting at the table in the room underneath the visitors' center—everyone except Chizu Sato, who was still crying in the bathroom, and a friend who was with her. Everything was all white and gray down there; it was like a hospital. Mr. Tanaka had left with the Americans, and a minute later that guy from the park left, too, so of course we started talking.

We should have just kept quiet. What was there to say? But really, really nasty things started happening. I don't even know how to describe it.

It started about the Americans. One of them looked tough and lean, like he had been in a war, but also friendly. The other one was younger and looked upset. He had tattoos. I'm so used to being tall that it's always weird around foreigners. But to me they both looked nice, like maybe they could help us. Other people didn't feel that way.

"Who wants to bet *they* had something to do with it?"

"They're U.S. Army. The army abducted Kari-*chan*."

"For experiments."

"Hey. You shouldn't joke about things like that," said Sumiregawa.

I was so grateful to him that I didn't have to say it. Sumiregawa the Genius. There was a guy you could count on. I tried to smile at him, but he wasn't looking at me; his eyes had gotten squinty like they did. He was always thinking.

"Guys, I told you," I said. "They're journalists. From a paper."

"What paper?"

"I don't know, but . . ."

"Where'd they come from?"

"They were just here," I said. "It had nothing to do with us. They're tourists, too."

"Is that what *they* told you?"

That question was asked by Mari Ogami like she meant it. Like not only did she think the Americans were on a side against us but she thought *I* was on their side, too.

"Mari!" said Koizumi.

Koizumi's my best friend. I know I can count on him, too.

A couple of the girls joined in—*Mari, what're you saying?*—but she kept staring at me. Finally she looked away.

I took a breath. It was easier to concentrate if I looked straight down at the table. "I didn't get all of it," I said, "but I think they saw Hiraoka, Mori, and Maeda before they—"

Then *everyone* started talking.

"Guys! Guys!"

"Shut up, Class Rep's trying to talk!" yelled Koizumi.

I went on, "Before they . . . you know. They're going to talk to the police. Maybe they can help us."

Then for a minute no one said anything. Somehow me, Sumiregawa, and Koizumi had done it. *Done it . . .?* It was like trying to put a genie back in a bottle. Without knowing why it was dangerous I had pushed it back in, and it seemed like it had worked. But in a minute it started all over.

People were looking at Michiko Kamakiri. She had been sulking all day—probably just in a bad mood—and I knew that wasn't what she needed. But she had told us she'd seen Kari, Mai, and Taeko all leaving the temple, walking down the road. I bet now she wished she'd kept her mouth shut.

There are girls where you look at them and think, they're beautiful. Then there are girls where if someone asks you whether they're beautiful, you'll think and say, yeah, they are. Michiko was one of those girls. Koizumi liked her. She was a nice girl, but she was too down on herself. I think she kept to herself too much. We were all friends in the class, but I guess some of us more than others.

"Kamakiri," said Koizumi, just trying to be nice, "what direction did you say they were walking in?"

Koizumi was keeping calm. I think he still thought we could find them.

"I already told you guys. South."

"But . . . you said north before," said Otsuki Sakura.

"I did *not*, I said south."

"No, I heard you; you said north for sure," said another girl.

"Okay, maybe I *did* say north but—it's not south *or* north; I don't know directions. *No* one here knows the stupid directions. I just meant like, *that* way. I was just thinking, like, that way was north, that was south. Then I got mixed up."

"So if you were like standing in front of the temple . . ." went Koizumi.

She broke out, "Oh what does it *matter*! They looked all over the place! They couldn't find them! Don't you guys get it? They're gone, *gone*!"

Then they were quiet. But any second someone was going to say something bad. I had to say something, or Sumiregawa did, but he was thinking again; I opened my mouth, but a girl said first, "You didn't like Hiraoka-*san*, did you?"

"You called her stupid."

"You called her a witch."

"Guys . . ." I started.

"So what?" said Koizumi, "We all say stupid things about people all the time." But he didn't say it loud enough.

"I heard you," said Mari Ogami. "You said it just today."

"So what if I did, huh?"

"You liar," said Mari.

What was *her* deal? She was just this quiet girl in the drama club. I mean, I thought I knew her.

Michiko looked at her. Girls can get so mad it's scary to look at.

"Liar?" she said. "Who's a liar? I said it; I'll say it again. Hiraoka was a stupid *witch*—and she probably jumped off a cliff because Su-God told her to!"

Then it just came out of my mouth; I couldn't stop myself.

"Kamakiri, you'd better stop talking like that."

Stupid. If I had just taken her side like I should have, they would have left her alone. But when I said that they knew it was alright.

"*You* did it," said Mari in a whisper. "Didn't you? And then Mai and Taeko . . . to get rid of the witnesses."

"*Witnesses?*" said Koizumi. "Ogami, *listen* to yourself."

Michiko jumped up.

"*That's right!*" she just about screamed. "I did it! I did it! I pushed that stupid witch off a cliff, or into a hole, whatever, and Mai and Taeko, too! I just hated her *that much*! I'm a murderer! And I thought you guys would just be *too stupid* to ever figure it out!"

Mari jumped up with her fingernails out like claws. Jin Sul-Kim grabbed her arm but he looked angry, too.

"Are you guys stupid or something!" yelled Koizumi. "It was a joke."

"Some joke," said a boy.

"Just get out of here," said Mari, Jin-*kun* still holding her. "I don't care if you did it or not. You were always a bitch and I bet you really *are* glad Kari's gone."

Michiko was crying and her makeup was running. She wiped her face and it left big stains on her cheeks.

A boy got up, saying, "Get someone; grab her! Get the guy who was here!"

Koizumi also got up. "You asshole, don't you know she was joking? Ogami, you seem awfully suspicious. Maybe *you're* the one." Then he added a kind of laugh, like he was joking, too; but that made it worse.

Michiko looked at me. I couldn't say anything. She knew just as well as I did it was all my fault. Then she swung around and pointed her finger at Keiichi Hirata.

"I'll tell you who it was. Who was the one who told us they were missing? *Him*. How would he know? That creepy, sick little jerk always liked Taeko-*chan*, and he stuck a pin through her like she was a bug!"

Hirata turned white and started to shake.

"You see that? He doesn't even have anything to say for himself."

But Hirata, who everyone called "Bug," couldn't say much at the best of times.

Muttering. Shifting. I felt like I couldn't move. Jin-*kun* was still holding Mari; Otsuki Sakura was holding his other arm, looking scared out of her mind.

"Hey, you freak," said Michiko, "tell me one thing. Did you rape her before you killed her, or after?"

Mari broke free, crawled onto the table, and grabbed her by the hair. I couldn't believe what I was seeing: like I said, a dream. Holding Michiko's hair in one hand, she clawed her face.

Jin-*kun* grabbed her again and Koizumi grabbed Michiko.

"Hey!" said Koizumi thinly. "Hey!" and he looked at me.

A boy had put his hand on Bug's shoulder just sort of because he had been told to, not knowing any better. Bug had started to cry, too.

I opened my mouth: "Guys . . ."

Michiko's cheek was bleeding. She pulled away from Koizumi and ran out of the room and the door slammed behind her.

I stood up. Right away everyone stopped talking. I knew if I'd just stood up before then . . . but I couldn't. I tried to talk, then realized *I* was about to cry.

Mari was still up on the table, on her hands and knees like an animal. Everyone looked at me.

Mr. Feng, the man from the park, came back into the room looking more scared than any of us, but no one paid any attention to him.

"Guys," I said, "how could you do this to me?"

To *me*? I don't know what I meant.

The last class trip we'd been on had been in our first year, to Hiroshima. I remember Kari standing and praying in front of the children's memorial, where they have all those paper cranes they made for Sadako Sasaki; I mean, we all tried to do *something*, but she was the only one who looked like she meant it. I remember the inscription on the plaque there from Sadako's classmates, who had it built: *Kore wa bokura no inori.* This is our prayer. I wasn't sure what to feel the whole time I was in Hiroshima, but I felt something then—*bokura*, us. I thought about our class. Being able to speak with one voice like that.

I went out through the same door Michiko had gone through, Koizumi followed me, then in a second Sumiregawa was there, too.

"I'm sorry," I said.

"What for?" said Sumiregawa.

"I'm just . . . sorry."

We were standing in a hallway. There was no sign of Michiko.

Koizumi had his hand on my shoulder. "Class Rep," he said, "this is crazy."

"I know," said Sumiregawa. "I mean, it's all in accordance with the principles of psychology, but . . ."

"Take your 'principles of psychology' to hell," said Koizumi. Then he added, "Sorry."

All three of us were shaking and sweating.

"It's all nonsense, right?" said Sumiregawa. "There's no conceivable way either Kamakiri *or* Hirata could have . . . ?"

"You tell me," said Koizumi. "You're the smart one. Hey, Class Rep. What do you think?"

"No." I shook my head. "No way."

"Really?"

I stared at him. I couldn't believe, after he'd stuck up for Michiko and everything, that he would even ask that.

"We're all friends," I said. "Nobody would do anything like that. Period."

And I believed it.

"All I know is, Ogami-*san* needs to be sedated," muttered Koizumi. "She started it all."

"Yes, she was the primary instigator."

"No," I said. "It's not anyone's fault. From now on we've got to be friends again." Then I thought about it and added, "Ogami is in the drama club. Maybe she's just gotten used to—kind of blowing up her feelings."

Then the door at the other end of the hallway opened. We froze. Mr. Tanaka came walking toward us, smelling like cigarettes.

We all loved Mr. Tanaka. He was a phys. ed. teacher, and it always seemed like he was on our side against the "educators" who were going on about molding us into "citizens" like it was still Meiji. He just looked solid and reliable.

"Boys," he said.

I felt so grateful. For a while it had seemed like we were all alone. But none of us could tell him what had happened; it was like our mouths were stitched shut. It seemed like he couldn't understand. I mean, *I* didn't understand.

"*Sensei,*" I said.

He gave me a really fake-looking smile as he went past.

When he had gone into the room, I said, "You two go back. You're my lieutenants—" Koizumi grinned at that—"I'm counting on you. I'm going to go find Michiko-*san.*"

I found her in a broom closet. I might have walked right by, but I heard her sniff.

I knocked on the door.

"Go away," she said.

"Kamakiri, it's me."

"Go away, Class Rep."

"Look," I said, "I'm sorry. It's my fault."

"Didn't you hear me? I told you I killed them. I killed your stupid girlfriend."

I leaned on the door. "Kamakiri—Michiko-*san*—I don't believe any of it. I think Kari and the others just got lost. I'm sorry, I just got mad for a second. I couldn't believe Ogami-*san* would say those things. I don't think she meant it, either."

"She meant it about me being a bitch. And *I* meant it, too. I mean, I *did* think Kari was weird, and I *do* think it's her own fault she's gone. But—I'm not *glad* she's gone. I wish she were still here and I could tell her I thought she was weird . . . and maybe she could tell me why she wasn't, or something. But I mean . . . I never talked to her."

Right then I really wanted to give her a hug.

I heard her sniff. "Okay," she said. "You can open the door."

I opened it. She was curled up like a ball in there, with the mops and brooms, and it was dark. For a second she looked scary, with her hair down over her face. I went in and tried to sit down next to her, but there wasn't much room. Then she kind of threw herself onto me, and I put my arms around her and held her as tight as I could. She was still sobbing but it was dry.

"You know," she said, after a while, "before the trip, if I thought this could happen, I would have given a million bucks."

"Huh?"

"Me in a closet with the Class Rep."

She tried to laugh, and I tried, too.

"I'm sorry I said bad things about your girlfriend."

"Hiraoka-*san* isn't my girlfriend."

"You really miss her . . . don't you?"

Her head was right underneath mine and I could smell the tears.

"Yeah," I said.

"You think we'll ever see her again?"

"I don't know."

"What *do* you think happened?"

"Like I said, I think they just got lost. It was dangerous. No one would do anything like that. It's all my fault—I never should have let everyone . . ."

"No," she said. "I mean really."

I thought.

"Maybe Kari didn't belong in this world."

It was something crazy to say. But it was what I had been thinking.

"I know what you mean," she said in a whisper.

Did she? Then she was crazy, too, to think what I was thinking. That for all I knew, on such a beautiful day, God himself had reached down and taken them—three pure girls—right up into heaven, to be angels or something.

"That's what I meant when I said it was her fault," said Michiko. "But I couldn't say it that way."

Kari, smiling. *Two people who've ever met can't* really *be apart*.

"Were you in love with her?"

"I don't know if you *could* be in love with her."

"This world," she said. "Stupid world. I'd like to just crumple it up and toss it out. Nothing makes any sense."

I started to get up.

"Don't leave."

"Michiko-*san*, I've got to go back."

"Just a little longer."

"I have to. *They* need me to."

"I'm totally in love with you."

Then right when she said it she blushed—and I could guess why, even though I knew she wasn't serious; not really.

The conversation we were having was so weird, so intimate. It could only happen because of what had happened, because of where we were. And we had both been saying the things we only ever think, whether we're serious or not (and how do we really know if we're serious?), and it had all slipped out.

"No, you're not," I said. "Well—I'm in love with you, too. But not like *that* . . ."

"Like Kari," she said. "Like how Kari was in love with people."

"Yeah."

She pulled back, and I saw her face and touched it.

"Your cheek okay?"

"It stopped bleeding."

I could see the cuts, but she had wiped off the blood. It didn't look that bad.

"You should put some iodine on it."

"I think I'll just let it scar up. Then whenever she sees me she'll remember what she did to me."

"Kamakiri, don't say things like that. We've all got to be friends now."

She seemed to think about it. "Okay."

"Let's go back together."

When she had stood up, she said, "I really *am* in love with you, though."

"Koizumi likes you."

She blinked. "Are you serious?"

"He's crazy about you. He said you look like an idol."

"Now you're just making fun of me."

"You should talk to him."

She was quiet. The suddenly she said, "You know why I bet Bug was *really* looking for Taeko-*chan*. He was going to confess his love to her."

"I bet you're right," I said.

Then she leaned on me and started laughing. "This is so crazy."

"I'm sorry." All of a sudden I wanted to tell her to forget those crazy things I'd said about Kari not belonging in this world. "I bet we will find them," I said. "Everything will be alright. You'll see."

Everything will be alright. That sounds like something somebody told me once.

Kari and I had drawn classroom cleanup duty, which was funny because the way our school did it was random—picking names out of a bucket—and as Class Rep, I did the drawing, so it was like a king getting executed for breaking his own law. Everyone laughed. I told Koizumi to grab a noodle sandwich or something and meet me in fifteen minutes because we always walked home together. He just rolled his eyes.

"What?"

"You're not telling me you're gonna pass up a chance like this."

"Hey!—Come on."

He knew I didn't like getting teased about that.

"Y'know . . . I bet you did it on purpose. Pretty smooth, Class Rep. But ain't that an abuse of power?"

"Shut up."

Kari was on the other side of the room, kneeling down as she wrung out the mop. She always got started right away.

"Look at those hips," whispered that jerk, my so-called best friend. "Can't say I blame you."

"Get the hell out of here."

"Alright, I'm going. You two lovebirds enjoy yourselves."

And he was gone, laughing.

Later, as we were putting the desks back in place, Kari asked me, "What was so funny?"

"Nothing. That guy's got a twisted sense of humor."

She laughed. "I guess so. But I like him anyway."

"I like him, too."

I leaned on the desk I'd just put down. Outside it was bright, but the blinds were half drawn and everything was really quiet and still. It was beautiful, like a scene from a movie. But I felt weird.

There were so many things I had to do every day, and a lot of them didn't matter to me. Sometimes it felt like I was just going through the motions. Even when Koizumi teased me, I couldn't think of anything funny to say back.

"What's wrong?" said Kari, tilting her head a little in that way she had, like she was trying to get a better look at you.

"Nothing."

I guess she didn't believe me.

"Hey. You want me to do *okiyome*?"

It's not my body that's sick, I thought, but I grinned a little. "Depends. Can you do *okiyome* on, like, a person's spirit?"

"Your body *is* your spirit," she said. Everything made sense when *she* said it. "Your spirit is everything about you."

"Um . . . well, okay then."

I shut my eyes.

I knew she wouldn't touch me. I could almost feel her hand there, a few inches away from me in the air. Then she said, "Tohru, listen. Your life is a beautiful story God is trying to tell. It might be hard, but everything happens for a reason. You just have to figure out what you're supposed to learn. I'll pray for you."

It was so strange: she didn't sound like herself. I mean, they were the kinds of things she would say; but for a minute it really sounded like someone else was talking through her.

I opened my eyes again. I don't know what I expected to see, but it was just Kari, smiling, with the light falling on her hair and turning it brown.

DETECTIVE HSIEN CHAO

Let's get one thing straight. I do my job and I'm good at my job. If I was chasing a murderer and he got trapped in a mudslide, I would risk my own life to pull him out so he could stand trial like he deserved. And I have done as much, in my day.

But if there's one thing I hate, it's undercooked tea eggs. And if there's another thing I hate, it's the Japs. I don't like Americans, but I hate the Japanese.

I don't like them coming here and throwing their money around, especially the tattooed variety, if you catch my drift. Just last month we had a boss who smashed a bar hostess's face with the butt of his gun because she wouldn't go down on him: he was supposed to be on vacation, but I guess old habits are hard to break. The Japanese cops came to take him, and one of them had the nerve to say to my face that it was our fault for selling them guns. It seems a few of them never got the message we aren't their colony anymore; or to be realistic, they know that wherever there's money, there's a colony.

My friends are old men like me and don't know what I'm talking about. They think it was good for us when the Japs were in charge. It was certainly better than under the Kuomintang with Chen Yi. But people are so shortsighted. They won't mind anything so long as it doesn't get in the way of their drinking.

It's true the Japs didn't kill too many children or rape too many women here, like they did everywhere else. We were their prize colony, and they wanted us to look good. My friends still remember what it was like (not me—I was born in '38, after the war had started, and I was too young to remember much even of that). But if you're a slave, what do you care if your master is good or bad? And when they had their war, their last insane war, we had been under them so long and they got us so whipped up that thousands of us went and joined their army. That army was tens of thousands of men marching to their deaths—for nothing. They say my father died in the Philippines before he could even shoot his rifle. Two of my uncles served, and only one came back.

The way I understand it, that war was a final paroxysm, like a dying man's. They'd gotten insecure, knew things couldn't go on, so they decided to destroy themselves and take thousands of us—and Koreans, and Chinese, and Okinawans, and Filipinos— along with them. If *you* want to die, fine, but maybe the rest of us are still keen on living.

I've talked with American veterans who say that no matter what else, the Japanese are brave. That isn't true. They're just so afraid of death they've made it into something beautiful. A man who really isn't afraid of death never thinks about it.

The way I understand it, it's because they didn't listen to Zhuangzi. I'm not much on Confucius myself, unlike my wife— I don't hold with all that *Book of Changes* hocus-pocus—but Zhuangzi took a practical view. Don't worry about a bunch of rules, he said, just mount on the Way and Integrity and go wandering in the boundless. That's not so hard, is it?

Zhuangzi said you keep all your money in a box with a strong lock to protect it from thieves. But if some eight-foot thief comes along, he just picks up the box and carries it off, hoping the lock *won't* break. So we're just hoarding things for the big thief. It's the same with people who hoard virtue. The Japanese kept all their virtue in a pretty box, and the big thieves just walked off with it; first the shogun, then Tojo, then the Americans.

Okay, the Taiwanese aren't perfect, but they're the best people I know—for honesty, for industry, and for kindness. The mainlanders are a mixed bag: there are some good ones and some bad ones, and because there are so many of them, I've met a lot of both. Americans aren't too bright—they don't have to be because their ancestors were—and they won't bother lying to "simple Asians" like us. The Japanese are as spoiled and devious as ever and I don't trust them, but if I had to, I would risk my own life for one of them.

We showed up at the gorge just as it was getting dark. It had been three hours since we had gotten the call; they wouldn't be happy, but what was I supposed to do when it took half an hour just to rout the call to the proper office? I do the job when they tell me and let the bureaucracy sort itself out, and I don't apologize for it.

My division is homicide, but I've been around a long time, and I can handle regular missing-persons cases when they're high profile: they know they can rely on me.

I was with my nephew Sheng, my sister's boy, from southern Kaohsiung. He was a country boy and a bit on the superstitious side, but he had a sharp mind. It was a bit late for it but I had never realized I was getting old. Then one day I was climbing a mountain and my left knee went right out from under me. I was in the hospital a month. That day I decided I would be retired within five years. I still had about three years to go.

I pulled up in front of the visitors' center. It gets cold at night in May, and I'd brought my trench coat. Sheng, the young fool, was in a box-cut shirt and trousers. I'd told him he looked like a grocery clerk.

"Hey, shop boy, where are my cigarettes?"

"Right here, Uncle."

"Where are my tea eggs?"

"Here, Uncle."

"Where are *your* cigarettes?"

"I don't smoke, Uncle."

Every time I asked him that, I hoped he would change his answer. I don't trust a cop who doesn't smoke.

It was already getting cooler. Everything around us was turning a red color. The birds and insects were out; pretty soon it would be intolerable.

People who come to Taroko Gorge and probably think it's beautiful don't realize how eerie it gets at night. I had been on a stakeout there—must be ten years ago now. When you're sleeping out in a tent, all the noises start to sound like just anything. You listen and you hear music—or voices, even familiar voices. I'm sure a boy like Sheng would say it's spirits, but I know it's just my mind playing tricks on me.

Still, the mind is a powerful thing.

The other three of us got out of the car behind me. Captain Zhao was in charge, a good man.

"Detective. What's the procedure?"

"Sheng and I will talk to the grown-ups. You and your guys will talk to the kids, then report back to me. I'll write down everything on my pad. Then Sheng will turn it into a report, and then someone else can come tomorrow and handle this."

The captain nodded.

The visitors' center was dark except for two windows on the ground floor. Feng, my old friend, had said they'd be waiting there. Then as we got closer, I saw dark figures on the porch—underneath the blue umbrellas where the tourists ate.

I held out a hand to Sheng, and he put a Paradise cigarette in my fingers. I held it out again and he put a tea egg into it. I love the feel of tea eggs in your hand—so smooth. We'd picked them up on the way, so they were still hot.

A man came down the stairs, and from his build I knew he was a foreigner. We met in the dark and he stuck out his hand.

"*Ni hao ma. Waw dzuh ji* Peter Neils."

"Your Mandarin stinks. What else do you know?"

"*She she. Omitofo.*"

"Let's talk English. You say you are Mr. Neils."

"That's right. I'm a journalist."

"Interesting. Who is your friend?"

There were three men with him, actually, and one woman. One of the men was Feng and the woman worked with him. Then there was one Westerner and one Asian.

"This is my friend Josh Pickett," said Mr. Neils. He nodded at a young bald man who looked very sick. He also looked strong. He was wearing a mud-colored tank-top shirt and I could see the muscles of his arms, coated with sick-sweat.

"Hi," said Mr. Pickett. "N-nice to meet you."

"And this," said Mr. Neils, "is Mr. Tanaka."

I shook hands with Mr. Tanaka. So he was the Japanese; the Japanese teacher. I didn't like the look of him. He was too young and too fierce.

"It's been two hours," he said in English.

"I'm aware of that."

"Where are the men? Where are the dogs?"

I started to peel my tea egg. "Would you like one?" I said. "They're warm. I think I have one for each of you. This is my nephew, Sheng."

"Where are the helicopters?"

"No helicopters. No dogs. Dogs in the morning. It's no use looking at night."

"See?" Mr. Neils told the sick American. "Like I said."

"This is ridiculous," said Mr. Tanaka. "I will complain to the embassy."

"I am sorry, but there is no way to do things faster. This thing takes time. Tonight we are here to talk."

I bit into my tea egg. It had been a good batch—not too salty.

"Would you gentlemen like a cigarette?"

"No, thanks," said the one called Pickett, his voice like a frog's. "I been smoking all fucking day, man."

"Are the children still here?"

"Downstairs," said Mr. Neils. And I wondered why this American—this journalist—heaven only knew what he was doing here—was doing so much of their talking.

Mr. Neils loudly slapped at his arm.

"Let's all go in," he said. "The bugs will eat us alive."

As regards this Mr. Neils, I should state my impression carefully. Mr. Pickett—his assistant, they said—I could see was a simple man, young and confused. But Mr. Neils. First of all he had a trim build, as if he had led an active life. Very wiry and skinny but his head was large. I found his eyes too big and even a little feverish. The way he talked was friendly, insinuating, and he was very ready to talk; he said too much too easily. That is often the mark of a guilty man.

There are, in my experience, two kinds of criminals: those who are very bad at being criminals and those who are very good. There is no middle ground. If Mr. Neils was a criminal he was of the second type; of the people I met, I found him the most suspect.

To begin with, he made a point of the fact that his assistant had dropped their camera into the river by accident. This camera supposedly had a photograph of the girls taken not long before they disappeared. It seemed clear to me, at least, that he was trying to put blame on his assistant, who was clearly under his spell, because he was all too ready to corroborate the story about the camera.

I wondered why they had taken a photograph of the girls in the first place. Who takes a photograph of strangers? That was too convenient.

The second point is harder to explain. I'm not one to jump to conclusions, and I know very well that people can seem suspicious not because they are guilty but because they are nervous people and afraid of being suspected. I can detect this sort of person. But Mr. Neils, with his friendly manner—trying to speak Mandarin, trying to calm down the upset Mr. Tanaka—was clearly not a nervous man. Yet he had certain characteristics of nervousness in that he talked too much. How to explain that?

Last of all, there was the way he talked about the girls. That is to say, he talked about them far too much. They had been strangers to him only a day before—why did he talk about them with so much detail, so much interest, so much apparent sympathy? It was like they were his own daughters. He was clearly fascinated by them. Why should that be?

As if to impress me, he talked about places he had been, in Africa and in Russia. He kept returning to the theme that there was something *in* this experience—his words—that he had perhaps not encountered before. And why should that be? Why was he telling this to me, a police detective? I admit the facts in the case were distressing, and even somewhat mysterious, but there was no reason that someone who had been to Africa and Russia should be so distressed, when—once again—he had never met those girls before.

As for Mr. Pickett, I interviewed him quickly. He seemed very ill and I felt pity for him. Strangely, he talked a lot about Buddhism, about the assignment they had been on before they had come here sightseeing. He asked me if I was a Buddhist. I had to say that I didn't consider myself one. He said that to him, that was alright, because to be Buddhist meant different things to different people. According to Mr. Pickett, we are all Buddhists; we are all on the path. I had heard the same thing from other Americans, and in every respect Mr. Pickett was ordinary. I advised him to get rest, and perhaps to see a doctor.

Mr. Tanaka was angry at being interviewed, as if he were suspected, when he was already upset with us. He smoked as I talked with him, resting his elbow on his knee and tapping the ashes into the lid of a soda bottle. I revised my first impression of him. For a Japanese he was manly, and perhaps in another circumstance, if his fierce attitude wasn't directed at me, I might have admired it. As things stood it grated a little, but the interview was soon over. He told me what had happened and I promised him dogs and helicopters in the morning.

When I suggested that it had been foolish of him to let the girls out of his sight for so long, he blew up at me and said that we Taiwanese were lazy, we never did anything by the book, and how could I tell *him* what was foolish? Then he took a puff on his cigarette and apologized. I was careful not to say anything. Like I said, I do my job. There was no point starting a fight, even over such a poisonous insult. How does that old song go? *It's less trouble for me and less trouble for him.*

Of course I had a brief word with Feng. He was incredibly distressed, predicting that his career would be over. He was the assistant supervisor of the entire reserve and he had worked there six years. I told him not to worry: unless he got on the bad side of the American reporter, his name would stay out of the papers. *I* was more likely to take the blame if things went wrong.

I had the facts. According to the captain, the students were very upset and frightened, but that was to be expected. They couldn't tell us anything beyond what the adults had, although a few of them offered elaborate theories—none of which the captain judged to be credible. Once again we were on the porch, and I had eaten three tea eggs and smoked four cigarettes.

I told Mr. Neils that I would call for buses to take them all back to Taipei. We would put them up in a hotel, at our expense, until the business was resolved.

"Get a bus for the students," he said. "We want to stay here."

Mr. Tanaka nodded. "We've talked it over."

"Have you all perhaps lost your minds?" I was eating another tea egg, and I asked this conversationally. "Where will you stay?"

"Here in the building. Mr. Feng says it's possible. There are food and beverages in the freezers from the café. The windows are glass and will keep out the mosquitoes. And Mr. Feng tells me they will close the park tomorrow."

"You are the teacher. Who will look after the children in Taipei?"

"We are not the only class; class C and class D are here also. Class D is in Taipei now. One of my colleagues will make sure my students are safe."

I thought carefully how best to dissuade them from this insane plan.

"Have you ever seen a ghost?" I asked Mr. Neils.

"I don't believe in ghosts."

"If you stay the night in the jungle—even in a building—you will see them."

He and his assistant shared a look. This superstitious Asian, they thought. They didn't understand that I was speaking figuratively, but it was the same either way. Past a point, what is the difference between the imaginary and the real? *You will feel as if you saw a ghost*. That will be enough.

"I hardly think we're afraid of ghosts, Detective Chao."

"Well, I'm afraid I simply can't allow it. It isn't legal. The park will be off-limits tomorrow, and that means off-limits to you as well, even though you are involved."

Then, as if he had done it a dozen times before, Mr. Neils reached into his pocket, took out a hundred-dollar bill, and held it out to me.

"What do you think I want with that?"

"Just take it. It's not a bribe—just for goodwill."

"What do you think I want with your dirty American money?"

"Take it."

"Do you think a Taiwan cop can be bought off with dirty money?"

"Please, take it."

I took his money.

"They're staying," I said to the captain as I went past him. "Get one bus for twenty children, as fast as possible."

It was entirely dark as we went to the cars, and Sheng lit our way with a flashlight.

In a low voice the captain asked me, "What do you think?"

I looked back to see the square shape of the visitors' center. Still two lights on. The foreigners had gone back inside.

"The girls took off their shoes to cross a stream."

"That seems right," said Sheng, eager to be heard.

"Be quiet."

"What happened then?" said the captain.

"The American reporter came out of the trees and raped and killed all three of them."

Captain Zhao was an older man, but not as old as I. His eyes widened.

"Do you really think that?" Sheng asked.

"No. It's just a theory."

"It's a pretty dangerous theory," said the captain.

"I know that. He's a foreign national. We could never touch him without hard proof. Hard proof means the bodies. They'll look for them tomorrow. But like I said, it's only a theory. I have many theories. Most likely it was just an accident, and those unfortunate girls are dead through no one's fault."

"But . . ." said Sheng, "even if it *was* him—all three of them? At least one would have gotten away, right?"

"Maybe his assistant helped him. You can hit one girl over the head with a rock and run after another. A second man grabs the third girl."

"You've been in homicide too long, Chao," said the captain.

I laughed. "You're right. Of course you're right. I must be wrong. I hope I am wrong."

The birds were still calling in the gorge. Once the night set in, it was more the insects than the birds. There were more kinds of insects than you could count in that jungle, more than all the perversions of human nature.

We got into the cars. There was one tea egg left in the paper cup, and I gave it to Sheng.

Michiko Kamakiri

We stood in the window and watched the bus pulling away: me, the Class Rep, Koizumi, and Sumiregawa. Outside it was dark, but the lights were on in the building and in the bus, and we could see them as they pressed on the glass and waved at us—like we were still friends, like Class Rep had said, and nothing had happened. But it looked like they were waving good-bye forever. I didn't want to wave back, and I looked around and saw that Class Rep and Koizumi and Sumiregawa weren't waving, either. So we all felt the same way.

Class Rep was staying because he was the Class Rep. Koizumi was staying because he was Class Rep's friend. Sumiregawa, I didn't know. I was staying because I didn't want to go back to the hotel with Mari Ogami and Bug and stupid what's-his-face who had told them to get the police or something before I could get away. But I made out like I was just worried about them because I had seen them last. I think Class Rep understood, though. Turns out he really *was* a nice guy—not just a "nice guy," like you say. If he hadn't come and said what he did, I probably would have killed myself.

I'd thought about killing myself a few times before—doesn't everyone?—and it was always when I was angry. When I was sad I just wanted to curl up and listen to some music. But when I was angry, I started looking at buildings trying to figure out how tall they were. *I'll show them. They'll be sorry.* I wonder if it's like that for everyone. . . .

So there I was, and it was all just so stupid. I was staying overnight, alone, with three hot guys and I couldn't even enjoy it.

Class Rep and Sumiregawa. Class Rep had said he was in love with me but not like *that.* I could tell he was sad and maybe he wanted to kill himself, too, but then when he talked it was like he was more alive. To be in that kind of situation. Alive and dead at the same time.

But Koizumi. He didn't *really* like me, did he? Class Rep was Class Rep and he was probably just trying to make me feel good.

Takeru Koizumi: the peacemaker. Grade: C-plus.

Not that I would be so thrilled if he did like me. Koizumi did judo and he was strong, but he was also a shrimp. He was even shorter than some of the girls; he was shorter than me. Also his ears were kind of big.

Whenever anything went wrong, like a fight, Koizumi was in the middle of it trying to patch things up. He really was the Class Rep's sidekick—like a deputy in a Western. He said it had something to do with judo philosophy, with the "peaceful reconciliation of opposites." Sure, like I had any use for *that.* What I care about is whether I have to lean down to kiss someone . . . you know?

But C-plus was my grade, too.

Why was I still making lists and doing analysis like that? I felt like I shouldn't be able to live, or laugh, or do normal things like that. But I was still alive and I couldn't help it. Koizumi was standing next to me at the window and I could see right across the top of his head. The flat top with the crew cut.

But I could think about it, and I couldn't. Whenever I started thinking about what I had been thinking about all day, I saw Kari and Taeko and Mai. And whenever I started thinking about them, and what had really happened, and what I was even doing there, I started thinking about Koizumi and Sumiregawa. Class Rep I *knew* was off-limits, but maybe I still had a chance with the ponytail.

A girl who was really on her game might have made the best of it: saying how scared she was, grabbing them, et cetera. But I didn't feel like that. The thing is, I kind of felt like I was one of them—brave, like a guy. Feeling like a guy, I said, "I heard them saying it gets really scary at night."

"I'm scared," said Class Rep.

"Me, too," said Koizumi.

Sumiregawa smiled at me. "Don't tell the other guys."

I laughed.

"We should leave the lights on," said Class Rep. "That way Kari can find her way back here."

Sumiregawa scratched his chin. "I don't know about that. I mean, if I were her, I wouldn't go anywhere. Who knows what kinds of animals are out there?"

Thinking about that, I shivered.

"We should still leave the lights on."

Okay, alright, said the rest of us. But then Sumiregawa thought some more and said, "Won't that attract animals here . . . ?"

"Who cares?" said Koizumi. "They can't get in."

"I suppose you're right."

It was like we didn't want to leave the window.

Mr. Tanaka came in. We were in the room on the second floor that had been the café, with the chairs turned upside down on the tables and an empty icebox. He stood in the door. There was a long way between him and us, and it just struck me how empty the place was now.

"*Sensei,*" said Class Rep.

Mr. Tanaka sighed. "I shouldn't have let you do this."

"*Sensei—!*" Koizumi and Sumiregawa started.

He put up his hand. "I didn't say I was going to make you leave. I just said I shouldn't have let you do it. There are lots of things I shouldn't have done."

He came in and sat down on the edge of the table, looking out the window. Class Rep went close to him.

"You're a good kid," said Mr. Tanaka, and his voice cracked a little.

"Sir, it wasn't your fault. I'll tell Mr. Hisegawa that." Mr. Hisegawa was the principal. "You were counting on me to watch them."

"No. I wasn't counting on you. I wasn't thinking at all."

I guess we all knew it didn't work like that. It didn't matter if Hisegawa blamed him or not, and he wouldn't fire him. Mr. Tanaka would have to resign, to save face.

"You were a good teacher," said Sumiregawa awkwardly. "I learned a lot from you."

Mr. Tanaka smiled. "You don't have to *lie*, Seiji-*kun*. I know I'm a blockhead P.E. teacher. Still . . . for a while there . . . it was a lot of fun, wasn't it?"

Then he wiped his face and went quickly out of the room.

A lady from the parks was staying with us, and she was really nice. All of the people I had met in Taiwan, including the policeman who'd talked to me and Bug, were nice. It's not like in Japan where they only pretend to be nice to you. Her name was Zhu, I think; she was young and had a ponytail.

She opened closets and found all kinds of stuff. She brought out cots, like in the army, and blue nylon sleeping bags. She put two cots in the room upstairs with the map, for the Americans, and one in the hall next door for Mr. Tanaka. Downstairs there was a storage room full of cardboard boxes, but with space on the floor, and down the hall there was a room like an office but empty. I thought that was kind of scary—I couldn't sleep in a room where there wasn't *any*thing—so the guys put down their sleeping bags in there, and I put mine in the room with the boxes. It smelled like dust so I left the door open. I don't know where Ms. Zhu was going to sleep.

To tell you the truth, I was kind of scared of sleeping alone, no matter what.

They had cut off the main power for the night, but Ms. Zhu brought out lanterns you could stand on the floor and some incense you burned to keep bugs away, just in case any got inside. We all already had some bites on our arms and they itched like crazy—so she brought out cream to put on them, and bottled water (Mr. Tanaka had said not to drink from the Taiwanese taps) and tea and instant coffee, *nori* crackers in little wrappers, and bars of soap—even though there was no place you could take a shower—and she left all that in a basket in the hall.

As we were getting settled, Mr. Pickett, the bald American, came down the hall asking if there was a bathroom with a "god-damn *normal* toilet" anywhere in the place. I think he was drunk, although I don't know where he could have gotten anything stronger than beer. I was walking past and he stopped me and asked if I spoke English. We were alone and it was pretty scary.

"L-little," I said.

"What's your name?"

"Kamakiri."

"That your first name or your last name?"

I didn't understand.

"Your *first* name or your *last* name?"

"Oh—last. I think last."

I remembered that in America it was backward.

He blinked at me. "Well, don't *you* go anywhere."

"I—I won't."

Then he walked away.

I'm not too good with foreigners. One time a guy asked me for directions, and he spoke Japanese and everything, but I got scared and ran into a convenience store.

I went back to the room where the guys were fixing their sleeping bags. There was a lantern in the hallway and another one on the floor of the room. They cast big shadows up the wall as they moved.

"I hope those Americans stay upstairs."

"Mr. Tanaka's here," said Koizumi. "He'll look after us."

"Well . . ." said Sumiregawa. "There *are* two of them."

I don't think any of us knew if we were joking or serious.

Sumiregawa was squaring his sleeping bag against the wall. I guess he was the kind of guy who liked to have things neat. When he was done he looked up and said, "I'll protect you, Kamakiri."

"Kamakiri's our little sister," said Koizumi. "She's got three brothers to look after her."

"But to tell you the truth," said Sumiregawa, "I'm a little of scared of the Americans myself."

"Mr. Pickett is drunk," I said.

"He looks kind of like he was in prison," said Koizumi.

"All Americans look like that," said Sumiregawa. "All Americans *have* been in prison at some point."

We all laughed.

Koizumi patted the floor next to him. "Come on in. You don't have to worry about *us*."

Class Rep was sitting in the corner with his legs pulled in. He didn't say anything. I came in and sat down, folding my legs to one side. Sumiregawa sat down, and after a second he took off his school coat and was in his undershirt. Then he took a book out of his bag, opened it, and started reading.

"Oh, come *on!*" went Koizumi.

"Hmm?"

"Man, don't you pay attention at those lectures they give

us? You'll never be a *member of society* if you be all antisocial like that."

"I'd much rather be well-read than a member of society."

But he was actually embarrassed, like he hadn't realized it looked weird. He closed the book and started to put it away, but Class Rep leaned over and read the title: "*Panseh?* What's it about?"

"It's French." Then Koizumi and I giggled because it sounded like *pantsu*, like, underwear. "It just means *thoughts*," said Sumiregawa.

Class Rep scratched his head. "Huh. Is it any good?"

"It's interesting. I could have finished it on the bus, but Sato kept wanting to chat."

I smiled to myself. He looked up and pulled on his collar.

"It's hot down here. If they don't run the air conditioning, we might suffocate."

"I know," said Koizumi, "and there's no windows or anything.— Hey, Class Rep. Say something."

"Something."

He and Koizumi both smiled.

Koizumi lay out full length, and I was kind of shocked, to tell the truth. I drew back a little. Right away he noticed and sat up again.

"This is like a sleepover," he said, "or camp. Should we tell ghost stories?"

"Oh, let's *not*," I said.

Sumiregawa stroked his chin. "Hmm, you're right. That would hardly be appropriate to these circumstances."

Koizumi reached into his coat. "How about cards?"

"I don't know; what games do you know?"

He grinned. "Egyptian Ratscrew."

"Igiputo Raaskuru?"

"It's an American game. My cousin taught me; he went to school in America."

"It's not Egyptian?" said Sumiregawa, sounding interested.

"I think that's just the name."

Class Rep finally spoke up. Curling his mouth a little, he said, "That's not a good game to play with girls."

Koizumi was shuffling the deck. He was good with his hands, I noticed.

"Ah, maybe you're right."

"Hey! I'm here with you guys, aren't I? I'm not scared. What is it, what is *Igiputo Raaskuru?*"

Shuffling the cards, with his little body like one of those actors in period dramas, he looked like an old-time *yakuza* dice roller. All he needed to do was take one arm out of his sleeve.

"It's simple. I deal the cards one by one. Being dealer doesn't give me any advantage, or not much of one. When you see a pair—like a three of clubs and a three of spades—slap your hand down. Then you get all the cards. The one with the most cards at the end wins. There are lots of rules you can make, but that's the simplest way."

"Who slaps their hand down?"

"Whoever sees it first."

"What if two people see it at the same time?"

He grinned. "That's the game."

Class Rep began to shift over. "No fair, judo boy," he said, trying to smile. "You've got fingers like iron. No one's going to slap before you."

Koizumi flapped his hand. "No way! If anyone's got the advantage, it's Kamakiri. You watch, we'll all be so scared of hurting her we'll never slap down."

It turned out he was right.

I was a little scared at first. A second into the game, Sumiregawa started sucking his fingers after Koizumi slapped him. He was basically out. Then there were two sixes, and I slapped down first, and like he'd said Class Rep and Koizumi both held back. I won a whole bunch of cards. I started leaning forward more. A few times one of them got in before me, but by the end I had twice as many cards as either of them.

"Hey, this is fun!"

"See," muttered Koizumi, "I told you."

"It's because of Kamakiri's skill," Class Rep said graciously.

"Never play games with girls."

"So what do I win?"

"Nothing."

"How about, loser has to do anything the winner says?"

"What would you make us do, anyway?" said Class Rep.

It's true, there wasn't much I could think of. Well, there were *some* things I could think of, but nothing I could *say*.

"I don't think I like this game," said Sumiregawa. "Let's play one that doesn't involve so much physical pain."

"Yeah, yeah, what else do you know?"

But Class Rep looked at his watch. "You know, actually, it's getting kind of late."

"Killjoy!" said Koizumi. "It's not even eleven."

Back at the hotel, we'd had a ten-thirty curfew. It was pretty early, but they got us up at eight.

All of a sudden there was a knock on the door. We all looked at each other, and finally Class Rep got up and opened it.

It was the other American, Mr. Neils. I thought he looked like Michael Keaton, but I was still afraid of him. He was wearing his what looked like an army jacket, and all the pockets were stuffed with these tiny packages.

"Hey, you fellas. *Shitsureishimasu.* You remember the temple you guys were at? *Asoko no otera da na?* Well, it turns out there's a monk who spends nights there, and he heard about us, so he dropped by to pay his—well, his respects, his condolences. Anyway, he brought us all some *moji.*"

We didn't understand all of it, but we knew that *moji* was Chinese for *mochi*—sweet bean cakes. We each reached out and took one. There were a whole lot of them.

Class Rep stood up and bowed. "Thank you very much," he said.

His English was pretty bad after all.

"Oh—don't thank *me*," said Mr. Neils, and scratched the back of his head. He stayed there a minute, looking around. "You guys having fun? That's good. That's good."

He nodded his head and shut the door kind of abruptly.

"He said something about a temple?" whispered Class Rep.

"A monk from the temple here," said Sumiregawa.

I started to unwrap mine; I *love* mochi. "The Taiwanese sure are nice, huh?"

I said before that I hate it when people do nice things you

don't ask for, then expect something in return. But sometimes they expect something, sometimes they don't.

"They really go out of their way for you," said Sumiregawa, "although—as in most cases—I suppose it depends on who you are. Still, I'm impressed. After all, they'd have good reason to resent us. . . ."

Koizumi raised one eyebrow.

"What, didn't you pay attention in History?"

"Oh—" said Koizumi, lamely. "Right. But hey, that was so long ago; and if Zatoichi and the One-Armed Swordsman can be friends, why can't Japanese and Chinese people get along?"

"Maybe if we got to know them better," said Class Rep, "the Americans wouldn't be so scary, either."

"I don't think I *want* to know Mr. Pickett," I said. "Maybe the other one is okay. What was his name anyway?"

"Nierusu," said Sumiregawa.

"*Nii-san,*" said Class Rep, and we all laughed because that sounded like "big brother."

"He's a big brother for all us," said Koizumi. "And Kamakiri's our sister."

There was a silence—but not like the ones there had been. It was kind of a happy silence. Koizumi lay back again, and this time I didn't act surprised. Looking at the ceiling, he said, "This is kind of nice, huh?"

"Yeah." I nodded.

"It is," said Class Rep.

"I'm sure they will find Kari-*san* and the others," said Koizumi—but he would have done better not to say anything.

There was another silence and it wasn't so happy this time. Class Rep looked away.

After a minute Koizumi opened his mouth again: "Are any of you guys religious at all?"

We all shook our heads.

"That's too bad. . . ." He sounded kind of sleepy. "Me neither. I thought, like, it would be cool if we were all different religions. Then we could all say prayers for Kari, just like . . . however we said them."

"And then," said Sumiregawa, "if it worked, we would never know which prayer had been effectual. Which was the true religion . . ." He yawned. "A most profound theological experiment."

Class Rep looked at his watch.

"You guys, it's past eleven."

"Come on," I said, but my heart wasn't in it anymore.

"No, we should get to sleep. I think we should get up early tomorrow. Otherwise the helicopters will wake us up."

"D'you think we'll get to ride in the helicopters?" said Koizumi, spinning one foot in the air.

Class Rep laughed. "Keep dreaming. Kamakiri, um—should I walk you back to your room or something?"

I laughed. "It's just around the corner and down the hall."

"But I mean, it's dark out there. . . ."

"Well, in that case—yes!"

The truth is, he was right. It was totally dark out there. And as I thought about it, I didn't want to leave. But I got up anyway.

Koizumi, from where he was lying, lifted one eyebrow.

"Be sure you come back, now. That's your own kid sister."

Class Rep flushed. It was kind of cute. "What d'you mean?"

"Forget it."

Sumiregawa was smiling. "Class Rep, you belong in a medieval tale of chivalry."

"Class Rep the samurai."

"Maruyama Tohruhito, the great standard-bearer of Lord So-and-So."

"Shut up," he muttered, and to me: "Okay, come on."

We went down the hall. Sumiregawa was right, it was getting hot down there and hard to breathe—but part of it must have been in your head because as soon as you started thinking about it, it got way worse. It was dark even with the lantern, and when we saw our own shadows I jumped.

"This isn't good. I'll be too scared to go to the bathroom."

"You could pick up the lantern and take it with you. That's what I'm going to do."

"Couldn't I wake you guys up?— I'm sorry, I'm kidding."

Then we were there. We were standing there and he started to turn, and I said, "What, aren't you going to kiss me?"

"Michiko-*san*, it's too late for jokes," he said.

"I'm not joking."

"Yes, you are."

"Okay, I am. 'Night."

"G'night." Then he added, "You know, I'm glad you stayed. It's more fun this way."

He turned and walked off: his big self, his bigger shadow.

There was a lantern in my room but I didn't turn it on. I lay down on the sleeping bag in all of my clothes and left the door open just a little so the air could get in. My head was just going round and round and I felt way too hot, but I wasn't about to get naked, not with all the guys around—and what if *Pickett* came in with whiskey on his breath still looking for a Western toilet? It felt like about six days had gone by in one day. I wanted to laugh and cry at once, so I just sort of squirmed around and hugged the sleeping bag.

I closed my eyes and tried to go to sleep. There was no way. It was quiet down there, not even a humming from the pipes, because the power was off. The boxes did make me feel a little better, though. They were like friends.

I kept thinking and it seemed like a long time had gone by. Maybe as much as an hour. Then there was a knock on the door and my heart went right out of my mouth.

I lay there breathing.

A whisper: "Michiko-*san*?"

It wasn't Pickett or the Class Rep. It was Koizumi.

"Hello?" I said.

Ba-dump.

"Hey. Can I come in?"

I was shocked because he sounded so casual, even though he was whispering. You don't just come by a girl's room at midnight sounding like that!

I got up and opened the door, and he was standing there, still in his undershirt.

"What do you want!"

"I just wanted to hang out some more." Then he looked confused. "I thought you did, too. Class Rep was just being a killjoy—didn't want to wake up Seiji-*kun*, either. He sleeps like a log."

"Okay, okay, come in. . . ."

I switched on the lantern. But it took forever because my hands were shaking. He plopped right down on the sleeping bag! Then he undid the top button on his shirt.

"Ahh. This is what the senior trip's all about. Right? I couldn't *believe* they made us go to bed at ten-thirty. We should have stayed up all night, like, drinking and singing karaoke and stuff."

I didn't get it. Usually he was so level-headed, so mature. But I guess I was usually different, too.

"I guess so."

"What's up, Michiko-*san*? You seem kind of scared."

I shook my head. "I guess it's . . . just the room; it's so dark down here and quiet. Plus it smells kind of rusty. I totally couldn't sleep at all."

"Oh. Me neither. Well, good thing I dropped by to keep you company, huh?"

"Yeah," I said. "Yeah."

"You're really good at Egyptian Ratscrew."

"Thanks."

For a crazy second I thought he was going to take out his cards again.

I was whispering when I asked, "So they didn't hear you leave?"

He shook his head. "I think they were both asleep."

"Hey." I moved closer to him. "Who snores?"

"Class Rep."

"I knew it!"

We laughed a little. Then I said (and I couldn't believe it), "So are you going to kiss me or what?"

He stared at me.

"What, do you want me to?"

"I don't know. Do you want me to want you to?"

"I don't know, do you want me to want you to want me to?"

"*I* don't know, do you want me to—"

Then he grabbed me and started sucking on my face like anything.

It was so weird. I mean I'd never had a *real* kiss, just a quick one with a boy in eighth grade who was too shy, and I kept imagining, what would it be like . . . and it *did* feel good, like I imagined, but then at the same time it just felt like two lips sucking on mine. The way you'd *expect* a kiss to feel if you thought about it. I guess it felt good in sort of the way it feels good to be tickled, and I didn't want him to stop. But then he did and hugged me like crazy and said, "I've liked you forever and ever and oh my God."

I guess I was supposed to say the same thing. It was too bad I couldn't—not exactly.

"Class Rep told me."

"He *what*—? That traitor!"

I was laughing. "Why? It's a good thing. Otherwise, I don't know, I might have just told you to go away. . . ."

"These are the delicate feelings of a young boy," he said seriously. "You can't just go—broadcasting them like that."

"It's a good thing; it's a good thing. Do it again."

One thing was for sure: we were both sitting down and it didn't matter at all that I was taller than him. Now I didn't mind that I was feeling hot and I put my arms around him. Then I heard something crinkle.

Ba-dump.

He pulled right back.

"What was that?"

He didn't say anything.

"Was it some of those crackers?"

"No . . . it wasn't some of those crackers." His throat was really dry.

"Show me."

"Michiko-*san*."

I punched him on the shoulder. "Show me!"

Slowly he reached into his pocket. He took out something a little smaller than a Post-It note. Red and shiny.

"Oh, wow. Oh, my God."

"I—" he said, and his hand closed around it.

"The whole trip?"

"The whole trip." Now he was really pale. "Hey," he said, "y-you never know what might happen . . . right?"

I wasn't looking at his eyes and I don't think he was looking at me.

"How can you like me?" I said. "I'm skinny and mean."

"I don't think you're mean. Or skinny. I like your face. You're really pretty, Michi—" Then he got up really suddenly. "I need some water I'll be right back I swear."

He walked out like he was limping. I sat there just like I had been sitting, not moving a muscle, and I heard his footsteps squeaking out into the hall and then coming back. He had a bottle of water in his hand. First he gave me some, then he spilled it all down the front of his shirt when he tried to drink. "We shouldn't be doing this."

"That's what *I'm* supposed to say! Close the door."

"Okay, okay."

He was holding the bottle of water and the *thing* was still in his other hand like he'd just forgotten about it.

Okay. He had been carrying that thing in his pocket the whole trip, while we were looking at cabbages in the museum, and on the bus. But before we left, *I'd* gone to Jusco and bought fancy underwear. Because you never know what might happen.

I started taking off my blouse.

"What're you doing?"

"What do you *think* I'm doing?"

"It's my first time," he said.

"What, you think it isn't mine?"

"I, I don't even know how to get this thing open."

"Well, how hard could it possibly be?"

"I—I mean, well, do you *want* to . . . ?"

"I don't know, dummy, do you want me to want—"

Then I heard his belt click as he undid it. I fell back like I was dead with my eyes closed. My clothes were still mostly on but I just couldn't look. And I felt his hands on me. He was kissing my chin, then my neck.

You were supposed to make noises, weren't you?—And what if I didn't make the right kind of noises, because what if it didn't feel the way it was supposed to?

Koizumi. I waited my whole life for this moment, and I didn't have any idea what it would be like. Do it to me. I'm ready.—Or something like that? I mean, it's not like I *watched* that kind of movie . . .

Then all of a sudden he stopped.

"What's wrong?"

"What do you mean . . . what's wrong?"

"Why'd you *stop*?"

For a long time he was quiet. I lay there with my eyes closed. Then he said in a really quiet voice, "Um . . ."

I opened my eyes.

"I kind of . . ." he said.

"You kind of what?"

"I blew my fuse."

"What do you *mean* you—oh. Oh."

"Yeah."

I would *not* look below his waist, but I said, "It's ruined, isn't it?"

"Yeah."

"Was it . . . was it the only one?"

"It . . . yeah."

He got up again. I lay there looking at the ceiling. I heard his footsteps again, and then in a minute, a long way away, I heard a toilet flush, and I lay there not sure if I wasn't actually really really relieved.

Then I was afraid for a second that he wouldn't come back, but he did, and he stood in the doorway and said, "Sorry."

"Close the door." He went back out and I said, "Close it from the *inside*, stupid!"

I buttoned my blouse back up. Everything else was in place.

"Can I just . . ." he said. "Can I just hold you for a little while?"

"Yeah," I said. "I think I'd like that. A lot."

He lay back down and put his arms around my waist very gently. At first I didn't hold him back, but then I put my arms around his neck, and it was nice.

"I like this," I said.

"I'm really sorry."

"Actually I think I kind of—I like this better."

"Me, too!" he said and he held me tighter. "Yeah, I—I was really, really scared."

"You *were?* Get out of here."

"No, really. Were you?"

"Yeah."

"But not anymore. Right?"

"No. Not anymore."

We lay there and after a while I turned the lantern off.

Then, after another while, he started to get up.

"I—I guess I should go back. It'll be weird if I'm not there in the morning."

"They'll get all kinds of ideas," I said, and laughed.

"Wrong ideas. But yeah, how would they know?"

"I don't know." I laughed again. "I mean when you think about it, it's really not that surprising."

"Really?"

"You know they say the first time is always like that."

Only one girl in the class, I won't say her name, I knew wasn't a virgin. That wasn't the way *she* had told it, but it was what everyone said who was old enough that you could trust them.

"I—I really do like you."

"I like you, too. But I have to think about it."

"Don't say no," he said.

"Of course I'll go *out* with you, dummy. I meant—just about this."

"Oh."

Then we both laughed.

"This is the craz*iest*," I said.

"Yeah. But I'm still really happy."

"Me, too."

Then it was later, and he had left. The sleeping bag was still warm and I was hugging it like crazy. I don't know how late it was. Also I don't know how it happened, when I kept feeling like I was going to explode, but I fell asleep.

Maybe it's true that whenever something really good happens to you, something really bad happens next—or the other way around.

Koizumi (*ba-dump*) had asked us if we were religious. Maybe I should have said that I pray to God all the time, but for stupid stuff. I guess if there is one religious thing I really believe in, it is that—I mean, that good follows bad and that what goes around comes around. Of course it's better to think about that when you're sad than when you're happy.

I have a boyfriend. He thinks I'm pretty.

I fell asleep and had a dream about Kari.

Only it wasn't a scary dream, not exactly. Nothing scary happened in the dream but it still *was* scary.

I just dreamed I was in some gray place, and there she was, in front of me. She was waving to me—but not *beckoning* or anything, not like telling me to come to where she was. Just waving hello—or I guess good-bye. But then she wasn't waving to me because it was more like I was looking at a picture, or a TV screen. I didn't feel like I had to wave back, like she could see *me* any more than a TV screen could.

I woke up and I was scared to death. I didn't know where I was and the boxes looked like people. Then I banged my hand on the lantern, and slowly, slowly, I got a grip on myself. I turned on the lantern, and just like it always is with nightmares, you're afraid there'll be something *there* when you turn on the light— but of course there wasn't anything. Just the boxes, and now, I saw, a torn-open red wrapper on the floor. I saw that and I laughed, and I felt a little better.

But there was just no way I was staying in there. I didn't want to go wake up the guys, either; it would be weird with Koizumi there. So I just put my lantern out in the hall, then dragged the sleeping bag out into the hall, then around the corner, then down the hall, and put it down in front of the guys' door. I lay down right there. It made me feel a lot better that Class Rep, and the ponytail, and my new boyfriend were asleep on the other side of the door.

I was still scared, but I could step back and *think* that I was scared, and not just feel it in my bones.

Hey, guys, I thought. *Your little sister is really scared right now.*

And then I wondered where Kari and Taeko and Mai were right then. *Right then*, at that moment—they had to be somewhere.

Didn't they?

PETER NEILS

Now, *my* brother Tom and I get along, but we've had our differences. That's only to be expected between people as different as the two of us. For the brief while, back around '90, when we were both in the States (during which time we collaborated in entertaining his parents-in-law), he fussed a lot of over my health. I resented the hell out of that for several reasons. First of all, what earthly right did he have to fuss over *my* health? I wanted to say, Who used to hold the thermometer under your tongue when you wouldn't stop squirming around? Who carried you home on his back after you got beaned by a fly ball at the Little League game? It just felt humiliating, him acting like he was my mother. And when it came to that, well, the years had taken their toll, and I had been living pretty hard for a long time, but I could still haul my carcass out of bed, and that's what counts. A person has a right to live his life how he wants to. But after he found me drinking out of an open bottle of Old English, he tried hard to get me to join Alcoholics Anonymous. I mean, he was polite about it, but that just made it worse.

He left pamphlets in my mailbox. Bet he didn't think I knew it was him, but I was watching through the blinds.

Now, I may be a drinker, but I do not have a drinking problem. When it's time to work I put the liquor away. That's what cigarettes are for. I have never in my life—well, except a few times—gone drunk into a situation where I knew I had to be sober. That's what it means to be a mature adult: to know when to and when not to.

This was apparently more than you could say for Pickett. But Pickett was young, and this was becoming more and more obvious.

For dinner, while we were still waiting for the cops, we ate cold sandwiches out of the café fridge: tuna-fish and ham sandwiches wrapped in plastic. There were beers, too, and me and Tanaka each had one, out of sight of the kids, but Pickett found a bottle of sweet plum liquor. I warned him to leave it alone, but I didn't have the heart to grab it out of his hand—not with him looking the way he did.

I ran into him after the cops had left, and he was drunk as a lord. He tried to hide it by not saying anything, but I could smell his breath.

I didn't say anything then. But not a minute later, when I was getting settled into our room, Ms. Zhu—the lady from the parks who stayed with us—came in looking terribly upset. She didn't even knock. According to her, Pickett was ranting all over the place because of the "retarded" toilets that were "all sunk into the floor." She didn't seem to realize he was drunk, as if all Americans behaved this way, but she asked me as a more reasonable American to go deal with him.

When I cornered him he seemed to think it was funny.

"Josh"—to emphasize what I felt to be his childishness, I called him now by his Christian name—"listen to me. We're not fucking around here. I can't be Crazy Pete anymore. I'm Peter Neils acting in my capacity as an investigative journalist, and this is business."

"You think I don't know that? You think I don't know *that*?"

"Those kids down there are looking up to us. You want to scare the shit out of them?"

"They're good kids, man."

"I know that. Do you want to—*corrupt* them with this bullshit of yours? Look at the Japanese guy. He can't be that much older than you, but at least he handles himself with a little fucking stoicism."

"Man, don't throw that word at me. I read Seneca."

"Look, just go splash some water on your face and lie down. We've all had a long day. And don't go making more trouble for these nice people."

For a moment I thought, Jesus, did my brother have to put up with this?—But no, I had never been this bad.

To his credit, he did what I told him. I didn't see him again for a while or get any more complaints. When I walked past an empty office, I heard him—apparently still on his *Apocalypse Now* kick—singing "The End": *"There's danger on the edge of town. . . . Ride the King's highway, baby. . . ."*

To tell you the truth, I wanted another drink myself. Instead I went outside and had one more smoke. There were only three Double Luckys left in the pack. I was still outside, slapping the bugs off my arms, when the monk showed up.

At first I thought it was some bizarre mirage. He came out

of the soup of the darkness, a big figure on a bicycle, wearing robes and—as most monks are, most of the time—smiling. The basket on the red ten-speed bicycle was filled with little wrapped cakes.

"Hello, hello! You spend the night here?"

"That was our plan."

He was a beefy fellow. He didn't give his name. He rubbed his hands together as he talked. "Of course I have heard about what happened."

"Thank you. This was very thoughtful of you," I said as I dubiously handled one of the cakes.

That superfluous generosity that was either a Taiwanese or a Buddhist characteristic, I wasn't sure.

Of course they give different reasons for it, but most religions have some central idea of giving. You could see that as evidence of an overarching divine spirit, but the skeptic in me has always wondered if it's only a way to rationalize some evolved need.

"The best thing," he told me, "is to keep happy, no matter what happens."

"Thanks. I'll try to keep that in mind."

Then, because it was sad to think that he had cycled all this way, through the insects and without even a headlamp, to receive such an indifferent reception, I asked him, "You live at the temple?"

"Yes!"

"Just you, or are there others?"

"Yes! Two other."

"How long have you lived here?"

"Six year!"

"Excuse me, then. Could you tell me, do you know if this sort of thing has happened here before . . . ?"

"Do you mean the disappearance?"

"That's right."

He thought about it for a minute, there straddling his bike. The question didn't seem to trouble him, just as nothing had troubled him so far. Finally he slowly nodded.

"Yes. These things sometimes do happen. People—go away."

"Do they get lost? I mean, are there things such as—I don't know, sinkholes? You know? Quicksand? Or holes that are hard to see, or hidden cliffs?"

He understood and shook his head. "No, they do not get lost. They go to the Pure Land."

Do you really believe that, I thought, or is it just skillful means, a naive way to make us poor bereaved souls feel a little better? But I looked at his face. There was no *uppaya* there, just an honest country priest. He himself, perhaps, the victim of it.

"Yes. The power of Omitofo is very strong here. Sometimes things happen that are very hard to explain."

"Can you, I don't know, think of any specific times this happened?"

"Yes. Ten year ago a lady disappear on top of mountain . . ." and he named one of the mountains in the range. "There is shrine. She stay there the night to recite Omitofo name. By morning she is gone. Nothing left, no sign. Everywhere, strong smell like flower."

"And this was before you came here?"

"Well, yes. But it was told me."

"Ah, thank you. Do you . . . well, do you think it might have happened again?"

"There is no telling. Power of Omitofo is very strong. Sometimes, yes, people only get lost. But paths safe. Sometimes things happen that are hard to explain."

"Thank you. Your English is very good."

He beamed. "Thanks very much. I never study. I learn from talk to people."

It was a lot better than my Mandarin at any rate. I thanked him again, helped him carry the cakes inside, and saw him off—that quixotic figure, that Taiwanese Friar Tuck on his bicycle.

There are a lot of stories in both Chinese and Japanese folklore about devotees who ascend to Omitofo's Pure Land, his heavenly realm of bliss. As I understand it, the Pure Land has a complex role in Buddhist theology, but most people basically understand it as heaven. A nice place to go where there are no cares, no bullshit. Sometimes I think it wouldn't be bad to have a place like that, although when it comes to the afterlife I find other visions more plausible. Sheol, a horrible Hebrew place of dampness. The something-or-other fields, gray and misty, where mediocre Greek souls went.

There is one Japanese story that I particularly like, about a hunter. According to the story, he was a mean, hard-living son of a bitch, but the moment he heard the preaching of a Buddhist monk, he shaved his head and set off for the Pure Land in the West. He went along calling, "Omitofo, Omitofo (or I guess in his case, Amida, Amida), where are you?" Then he finally got to the coast of the Pacific. There when he called, a voice came out of the sea, saying, "Here I am." And he died there, and a lotus flower grew out of his mouth.

I thought that was pretty neat, but I didn't think it was what we were dealing with. Myths are great, but they're just that. *Some things are very hard to explain*, the monk had said, and he was right, but a supernatural explanation is just another explanation. *Deus ex machina.*

I chatted a little with Mr. Tanaka when I dropped by to give him his *moji*. There were twenty-nine of the damn things, and I figured we were going to be eating them for the next few days.

"That detective was an arrogant cocksucker," he said in Japanese, as much as the mild Japanese language allowed him.

Privately I agreed—and I was astounded because it was a Taiwanese type I had never encountered before—but I said, "Well, he has his facts anyway. Now all he has to do is get the dead man's testimony from a medium." As a Japanese I thought Tanaka might get the joke, but he only squinted, so I said, "Never mind."

When I got back to our room, the room with the map, there was no sign of Pickett. I had set up both our cots by the wall; his bedding was all laid out for him. The place had a roomy feel, like a penthouse with all the windows. I took a flat part of the map as a desk and sat down.

It was time to think.

I took out my notebook—with the black-and-white marble cover, the kind I had used in school and through my whole professional life—and started to write down the facts of the case as I knew them. There was a lantern in the room, and outside it was completely black. When I looked up I could see myself in the window, behind the miniature hills and valleys of the Taroko reserve.

facts in the case

I wrote.

3 missing, female
last seen probably between 2:30 and 3, May 21, 2000

That was a pretty big window of time, but I couldn't safely get it any closer than that.

clues:
3 pairs shoes, socks rolled up in shoes

And come to think of it, where were the shoes? Had Mr. Feng given them to the police? There was a lot I didn't know, and I didn't fully trust the cops to keep a handle on it.

theories.
1. they fell into a hole.

That sounded so inelegant, but it was better than fleshing it out with the visual details my imagination was only too ready to supply.

2. they fell off a cliff, possibly into the river.

That seemed unlikely. If they had really gone into the river, more than likely someone would have seen the bodies.

3. *they simply got lost and are still out there somewhere.*
4. *they were taken up into the Pure Land.*

When I'd started writing I hadn't been aware of any noise. As time passed—I'd taken off my watch, and it was ticking there next to the notepad—and the spaces between the scratchings of the pencil grew longer, I started to notice it.

It was muted by the glass and I knew if I were outside, it would really be something. Birdcalls. Branches creaking. The river—you could hear it if you listened, hissing like a gigantic snake. Other cries of what might have monkeys, that sounded disturbingly human, but it's not like I was a kid.

Then, I will swear to my dying day, I heard a woman's voice.

Water, water, water, she said.

Or possibly: *Daughter, daughter, daughter.*

Now, I know there must be some explanation—but if it was a birdcall, it wasn't any bird I knew. At the Fo Guang Shan temple there had been birds, mynah birds, that could imitate human voices like parrots. *Omitofo*, they said. *Ni hao.* The monks were very proud of them.

I sat there for a second, telling myself not to imagine stupid things. Then I swore, got up, put on my jacket, grabbed the flashlight Ms. Zhu had left for me, and went out on the porch. I splashed the light around, and something shot into the undergrowth and just about gave me a fucking heart attack.

I had left some of the bug-repellent incense burning there in case I went out for a smoke, and they didn't get me right away. I stood there for a second looking at the thick darkness. It stopped exactly at the beam of my flashlight—wouldn't even give me an inch. Away from the city the stars are usually brighter, but here they were just a vague haze that gave no light, and the moon was behind a cloud. I wondered if the clouds meant rain.

I waited, and I didn't hear it again, although the creaking and hooting was now so loud that it finally drove me back in. I took off my jacket and sat back down. I looked up and saw my own face and jumped, then gave myself the finger for being such an idiot.

Your own reflection can be a weird thing, especially when you haven't seen it for a while. For a second it could be anyone.

5.

It was finally time to write what I didn't want to write. But I thought of something that let me put it off for one more minute:

5. *one of the kids did it.*

It wasn't so hard to imagine. A jealous girl or a boy with a twisted mind. Mr. Tanaka had made the three girls out to be blameless, but loss always sentimentalizes; or quite possibly someone had hated them exactly *because* they were blameless.

It scared me, though, that on instinct I just wrote *did it*— that as much as my conscious mind wouldn't admit it, I had been thinking of it so long that of course I knew what I meant by *it*.

6.

I wrote. Then two heavy hands came down on my shoulders and I screamed right the hell out loud, and when I saw his reflection behind me I screamed again. Fuck!

"Pickett, Jesus fucking Christ, you scared the living shit out of me. Didn't your mother ever teach to knock, you son of a cocksucking whore? Sorry. I'm sorry I yelled at you before. Sit down; keep me company. I think I'm losing my mind here."

He looked like he had sobered up, and I was glad. He sat on the edge of the map.

"What you got there, Crazy Pete?"

I showed him. He looked it over, nodding and going, "Huh." Then he said, "What's number six?"

"I don't know. I don't have a number six yet."

"Yeah . . . it's a bitch."

"I know. Maybe I'd better leave it to the police," I said.

I stood up. Mainly because I didn't like him being so much taller than me, sitting up on the relief map.

"Have the kids gone to sleep?"

"I guess so. I was down there, and I didn't see 'em."

"What about Tanaka?"

"He's still up. He's out on the other side. Motherfucker's smoking like a chimney."

Somehow that made me feel better.

"What about you; how are you holding up?"

"Not too bad, not too bad," he said, sort of nodding his head in a grotesque parody of the ordinary conversational bullshit.

I looked at my watch. It was about ten to midnight.

"Seriously, man. I know this is hard on you."

"No, really, I'm alright."

I paused. "Glad to hear it."

"How 'bout you?"

"Well, like I said, I think I'm losing my mind. I think I heard a woman out there just now. Like an older woman."

"Oh, yeah? What was she saying?"

He sounded altogether too casual.

"Either 'water' or 'daughter,'" I said. "I wasn't sure. But hey, I know the shit was in my head, I'm just saying."

I ran my hands down my face.

"'Water,' huh?" said Pickett.

"I'm telling you, man, I'm just losing it. Maybe I should get the fuck to sleep, huh?"

He looked right at me and, with every appearance of being sober, said, "You think I killed those girls, don't you?"

I took a full step back from him. Held up my hands. "Whoa. *Whoa.* Time out."

He repeated in the exact same tone of voice, "You think I killed those girls. Don't you?"

The way he sounded and looked was almost sad, oh, Jesus, he was still drunk off his ass, I knew it.

"Pickett, I do not fucking think that for a second. Come on."

"See, see," he said immediately, pointing his finger, "I knew, I *knew* you would say that—because see, if you didn't think it, man, you'd have been like, *What the fuck are you talking about?*— but *you said* you *didn't* think it, and that means you did."

"That is some fucked-up logic. Examine it."

"You think when I went off, I just ran after 'em, ran 'em

down," he counted on his fingers, "fucking raped them, fucking killed them, fucking threw their bodies down some hole."

"I do not—no."

"Man," he said, shaking his head, rocking back and forth on the edge of the map, "I went in the bushes, I took a piss, then I puked my fuckin' guts all over the place. I was gone maybe fifteen minutes. Then when I came back you were taking a snooze. Fuck, man, I could probably *show* you the puke."

"Pickett, there is no need to fucking show me anything because I do not for a second believe that you had anything to do with it."

"Nice try," he said. "But I know, *you told me*, you lied to that Japanese dude before. So I know you're lying to me now."

Still his tone was so goddamn mild.

"Pickett—look me in the eyes. Look me in the fucking eyes. *I. Do not suspect you. Of anything.* So just chill the fuck out."

I suddenly realized that *without being at all aware of it*, I had been walking backward the whole time. And that I had somehow managed to put the map between me and him. He had twisted around to look at me. And we stood there.

"Man . . ." No doubt about it, he was drunk, and now I thought he was going to cry. "You are the only person I trust here," he said, "and you don't trust *me*—"

The last word was cut off as he started to wail.

"Shh," I said. The only thing worse than this shit would be if somebody overheard. "Shut up."

He clenched his jaw and all that came out was an awful gravelly moan.

"Thank you," I said.

Then I began to walk back around the map toward him. He sat there looking at me with his wet eyes like an overgrown child.

"Pickett," I said, "I swear to fucking Jesus Christ. I swear to the Buddha. I do not, nor have I ever, thought you raped or killed anyone. I know you are a fucking stand-up guy and you're my friend and I do, *do* trust you. So okay? Come right down off this shit. Because quite honestly . . . it scares the hell out of *me* to see you like this."

My voice was shaking a little, too, by the time I finished.

He lunged forward and threw his arms around me.

"Oh thank fucking Christ, man."

I put my arms around him, too. "I see now how you thought that. Okay. I see it. But we're good now. I'm glad you told me. It has to be like this."

"I was scared, man," he said. "I was scared to death."

"It's fucking alright. We're in this together."

And so on, and so on.

Finally he left—maybe to go cry some more, maybe to drink some more, I didn't know. When he was gone, I sat back down.

It was time to be honest with my sack-of-shit self. What did I think?

I thought the chance that Pickett had killed those girls was like that mathematical function that infinitely approaches zero but never reaches it.

It was almost certainly true that he had only been gone ten or fifteen minutes. It was almost certainly true that all he had done was pee and throw up. For all he knew, by the same logic, *I* might have done it while he was off puking in the bushes. And besides, there were people. If there had been screams or anything, wouldn't someone have heard?

He'd said he didn't have any interest in fifteen-year-old girls and I believed him.

But. We all have moments when we aren't quite ourselves. I know that as well as anyone.

Pikketto! said the girl.

And the fact was I didn't know the first thing about Josh Pickett, aside from what authors he had read and what drugs he had taken in college, and how was I supposed to get anything from him now? When I didn't trust him.

Let's be honest. Do I have the slightest sexual interest in young girls?

Of course I don't.

When I saw those girls, could I honestly say that no sexual thought entered my head?

Of course I couldn't.

The truth is that we don't know what we want until we want it.

TOHRU MARUYAMA

I **woke up** to the quiet. Usually it's a loud noise that wakes you up, but lying there, it was like it had gotten so quiet that I couldn't stand it anymore. It was weird, but I knew right where I was and everything. It felt like I had just closed my eyes for a second.

It was still dark, but somehow I knew it had gotten light outside. I looked at my watch: eight-thirty on the dot, the time I would have had to get up anyway. I guess my internal clock is just that good.

I couldn't remember if I'd had a dream the night before. That was good. Unless—I might have had a dream about something good.

Koizumi and Seiji-*kun* were still asleep, rolled up in their sleeping bags. It had gotten colder during the night. I didn't want to wake them up, so I put on my shoes carefully, got up carefully and slid the door open and slid it closed again. I felt like taking a walk.

Right outside the door on the left, Michiko-*san* was sleeping. I wasn't that surprised to see her. She looked cute when she was asleep. She had gotten all tangled up in the bag, and she had this annoyed expression on her face.

I got some tea and some of the crackers from the basket in the hall, and I ate the crackers as I walked. There was a thing that gave you hot water in the kitchen, and even though the power was off, there might be some left from the night before. A lot of kids in the class bragged about drinking coffee, but I always liked tea.

Upstairs the light came in from everywhere. Only it wasn't bright. It was like miso broth, kind of drifting in through the windows, and everything was so still and quiet.

I got a shock to see Mr. Tanaka sitting there, motionless, on his bed in the hall. When he heard my footsteps he looked around, and I saw the circles under his eyes.

Koizumi had slept at my house before, but it was strange to wake up with someone you had only ever seen in class.

"*Ohayou,*" he said.

"*Sensei?* Are you okay?"

He shrugged. "What do you think?"

I got the feeling he hadn't slept at all.

"Maruyama," he said, "don't ever smoke. It's a bad habit that kills you."

"I won't, sir."

I knew that Sumiregawa already smoked on the sly, but maybe he needed something like that to think as much as he did.

We were looking out the window. The way the light was, it looked like it was scattered everywhere, hanging in flakes on the trees and rocks. The sky was full of pink clouds that covered the sun.

"Maruyama, you're a Morioka boy. You've been a city boy your whole life, haven't you?"

"I guess so, sir."

"Well, I grew up on a farm. In the Tono boonies. You know what it means when the air gets still like this?"

I guess I hadn't realized how the air itself was still. But even outside, there was no noise, and we could see the tree branches hanging there.

"Even the birds are quiet," said Mr. Tanaka. "It's going to rain."

There were some birds, but it was nothing like yesterday. When you did hear them they sounded lonely, like they didn't get the general plan.

"You think so?"

He nodded. Then he said, "Typhoon."

"No way."

He just rolled his jaw.

I was thinking, no way could there be a typhoon. There was bad luck and then there was just the kind of thing that made you want to roll up in a ball and close your eyes. But maybe he was wrong. I'd ask the parks lady; she would know.

Before we'd left, they'd warned us about the water, we'd had to get shots, and they'd warned us about typhoons. You get them in Japan but not much in Morioka; more near the ocean. And since Taiwan is an island, I guess all of it is kind of near the ocean.

On the bus when we were driving through town, the girls had all laughed about how ugly Taiwanese buildings are. A lot of them look like big squares made out of bathroom tiles. But Sumiregawa had explained that they were built that way on purpose because when a typhoon hit, houses like that dry off quickly.

"But sir . . . wouldn't they have known about it last night?"

"You can't ever predict the weather. That's one thing I know."

I started to pace around.

"You know what I like?" he said.

"What, sir?"

"Fishing. I wonder if you could do some good fishing here. You ever been fishing, Tohru-*kun*?"

"No, sir."

"That's a shame. Kids these days don't *do* much, it seems to me. Not that I'm so old. I'm thirty-two."

"I think Koizumi's been fishing, sir."

"Go make your tea," he said.

"Sir . . . do you want anything?"

"No, thanks." He smiled and said again, "You're a good kid."

A good kid, maybe, but all the same I felt like I couldn't *do* much.

Then just as I was going he called to me, "Maruyama. You liked Hiraoka, didn't you?"

"S-sir?"

"I could see it in your eyes. Well," and he took a drag, "I don't blame you. She is special."

I just stood there looking away.

"These schools," he went on, "they're trying to turn you into a bunch of machines. But a girl like Hiraoka is different. They'd never get her, no matter how hard they tried."

When I went back downstairs, Michiko had gone off somewhere. I wasn't too worried about her now. Seiji-*kun* was still sleeping and Koizumi was standing there with his hands in his pockets, like he was thinking.

"Oh—hey, Class Rep."

"*Ohayou*, Koizumi."

We'd been friends since fifth grade, but I had never gotten past calling him by his last name. It just sounded fancy, like a title.

"You sleep good?"

"Yeah," I said. "I was surprised."

"Me, too." Then he looked at Sumiregawa. "You know, for a second I kind of thought he was dead."

Sumiregawa didn't even snore as he lay there. With his long hair down, he looked like a girl. I smiled. "He's recharging his batteries."

"There's an open tap out back," said Koizumi. "I feel all gross. I was going to see if I could take a shower or something. Want to come with me?"

"Sure."

I think if Koizumi had fought in the war, he would have been the life and soul of his squad. Even if they were trapped on an island or something and had to kill themselves, right until the last he would be going around cheering everyone up. He could always say something *normal*. How can I explain why it made me happy, him talking about a shower?

"Say," I said, "You know where Kamakiri went?"

"Beats me. That's her bag there, isn't it?"

"I guess she got scared during the night."

"Don't blame her."

As we were walking he said, "Class Rep, umm . . ."

"Hmm?"

"I kind of made my move last night."

We both looked straight ahead as we walked.

It didn't have anything to do with me. All the same, it made me feel kind of weird to hear it—kind of hot inside. But kind of happy, too, and I smiled.

"Good?"

He swallowed and nodded. "Yeah."

"You know, I told her yesterday."

"I know; she told me you told her." Then he slapped my arm. "And hey, what was up with that?"

"Kamakiri was feeling really down. You know," I said, "I think when you like a person, you think they know it. But they don't always. I mean, she really had no idea."

He scratched his head. "I guess not."

"Hey, Koizumi . . ."

We'd reached the door, and I stopped.

"Huh?"

"Did you," I said, "well, did you use it?"

He looked shocked and put his hand on his chest.

"Class Rep! And here I was thinking we knew each other. You think I'm the kind of guy who would take advantage in a situation like this? Honestly! We were just getting to know each other. They can say what they like about modern youth, but I'm old-fashioned the whole way. I think young people should think hard before they make these decisions."

Then why did you pack the thing, I thought. But I only smiled. "That's good. I don't think it would've been a good idea, either."

"Honestly, even suspecting me of a thing like that."

"Kamakiri's a good girl," I said. "You take care of her."

He touched his chest again. "Count on me!"

If it was really going to rain, it still hadn't started. It was hot and damp outside, but it had been hot and damp yesterday. Before we even got around to the back of the building, we heard a splash of water and froze.

I peeked around the corner. I could see the top of a blond, crew-cut head. It was the American Mr. Neils, and he'd had the same idea before us. He had gotten laundry frames somewhere and pulled them together, with sheets hung over them, to cover him while he dumped buckets of water from the tap over his head. The water was leaking out from under the frames.

"*Oi!*" called Koizumi. "*Ohayou, Gaijin-san!*"

Mr. Neils spit out water and called back, "*Oi, ohayou, Nipponjin-san!*"

Uh-oh, I thought, he speaks Japanese. Of course he'd used a few words the night before. The thing is, it isn't exactly polite to call someone a *gaijin*, or foreigner, but Mr. Neils didn't seem to mind.

"Shit," muttered Koizumi, thinking the same thing. Then he called, "*Nihongo wakaru kai?*"

"*Iie, iie, chotto dake.*"

"*Ahh, wari naa.* I didn't mean to call you a foreigner."

The frames came up to his nose and we could just see his eyes; he looked like he thought it was funny.

"That's okay, I am one. Anyway, we're all *gaijin* here. What brings you guys out?"

His Japanese was actually pretty good, and he spoke casually, which was a relief. Sometimes he dropped back into English, but mostly I understood him.

"Same thing as you," I said.

"Hey," said Koizumi, "can we come in there? That was a good idea with the sheets."

"Sure thing—that is, if you don't mind it."

Looking around to make sure Kamakiri or the parks lady weren't in sight, we stripped down quickly and got inside. There was just enough room for all of us. We hung our clothes over the frames.

"No peeking!" said Koizumi. "We can't help being Japanese."

Me and Mr. Neils laughed. It's like I said: in a situation like this, you say the things you would always think but don't have the guts to say.

We took turns filling the bucket and rubbed our bodies with soap. It felt really good.

Of course I didn't peek, but I could see Mr. Neils's chest. It was covered with hair like a wool blanket. I think me and Koizumi had about ten chest hairs between us.

When we were finished, we wiped ourselves on the sheets and got dressed, everything except our socks. We went and stood in the sun to finish drying off, our feet in the grass.

"Now," said Mr. Neils, "that was efficiency, guys. I don't know why they're so damn uptight in America."

"I've heard that," I said. It was hard to imagine. In Japan parents take baths with their kids until they're pretty old.

Anyway, if we had been scared of him, we weren't anymore. It's hard to be scared of someone after you've been totally naked with them.

"Hey," Mr. Neils said suddenly, "you guys know a song?"

"Sure, I know a bunch of songs," said Koizumi.

"It goes like, well—" and he started to hum. "Sorry, I don't really have the words."

It sounded kind of familiar, but . . . "No words at all?" I said.

"Well—*sarabai*?"

"Oh, 'Sarabai'!" said Koizumi and started to sing, "Hop, hop, hop, hop, hopping all around, how *are* you . . . ?"

"That's right," I said. "It's an old song, like 'Sakura' or 'Yuki wa Kon-Kon.'"

"Hmm."

"What about it?"

"Well, it's just I heard your friends singing it, when—well, you know."

Koizumi gave a kind of sad smile. "Taeko-*chan* really likes that song."

"It's hard to imagine," and the name caught in my throat, "Kari singing it, though."

"Well, she'd do anything to make someone else happy."

"That's right."

"Anyway, I was just wondering if it, you know, meant anything."

Koizumi shook his head. "Not a thing. It's total nonsense." *Sappari imi ga nai*, he said.

"Yeah," said Mr. Neils, and he shook his head, too. "That's what I thought."

"Good evening. Mr. Round Moon, how *are* yo-ou. . . ." Koizumi sang softly.

"You guys are in your last year of junior high, right?"

"Yep."

"You going to a good high school? You get through Exam Hell alright?"

"Man," said Koizumi, "you know a lot."

"It wasn't so bad," I said. "The *real* Exam Hell is for college."

"We got into a pretty good one," said Koizumi. "It's in Sendai. Y'know, Class Rep could've done better, but he dragged himself down for me."

I laughed. "You know that isn't true."

Still, I was psyched that I could go to high school with Koizumi. Jin-*kun* was going to the same place, too, because he'd asked me for advice on where to apply, but Sumiregawa was going straight to the top. And . . . Kari had been going somewhere else, too.

We were sitting down by then, on the hillside. Not too many bugs. For some reason it didn't feel bad just to sit there peacefully—maybe because Mr. Neils was there and he didn't seem worried. At least not on the outside.

"Nierusu-*san*," said Koizumi, "you're a reporter, right?"

"Well, sort of, yes."

"So did you break some big stories or what?"

"Well . . ." He squinted into the light. He had a kind of, I don't know, an expressive face. It screwed up whenever he talked. But maybe all Americans are like that. "I've been in a lot of places, but the news is always somewhere else. And sometimes you see things, well, things you're not supposed to report on."

Koizumi looked impressed. "You mean like *cover-ups?*" he said in English.

"Yeah," said Mr. Neils. "Like cover-ups. What do you guys want to do when you grow up?"

It was hard to think about that right then. I could talk—in fact I liked talking—about just ordinary stuff, but I couldn't think about anything serious. A part of me felt like I had always been there, at the gorge, and I wasn't leaving anytime soon.

"I dunno," said Koizumi. "Maybe a teacher or something. I never really thought about it. Class Rep?"

I shook my head.

"I bet Class Rep will be prime minister."

"Ha, yeah. No way."

"Maybe you could be a reporter," said Koizumi.

"I don't know if I'd recommend that," said Mr. Neils. "It's not for everybody."

Traveling all around the world. It sounded exciting. But that was what we were doing now, wasn't it, and already something bad had happened.

"Listen," said Mr. Neils, "you guys are pretty brave to stay here. I'm impressed that you care about your friends like that."

Actually what he said was *moved*, but I guessed he meant *impressed* because guys don't say things like *moved*.

I didn't say anything. Koizumi looked embarrassed and scratched his head. But Mr. Neils went on, getting kind of worked up, "You know, sometimes I think nobody gives a damn about anyone in this world."

Then I heard the door open, and Ms. Zhu came walking toward us. I don't know where she had slept that night—she was just *there*, like a helpful spirit. A really small, smiling lady spirit.

"Good morning," she said in English. "Did you have a good sleep?"

Mr. Neils got up quickly; I think we were all embarrassed by our bare feet.

"Yes," he said, "very good; thanks very much. We're really sorry to trouble you."

"No trouble, no trouble. But I come to tell you—it's bad. I listen to cordless radio. They say . . ."

No way, I thought.

"Typhoon."

"Typhoon?" said Mr. Neils, leaning forward and squinting. He couldn't believe it, either.

"Very big rainstorm, sir."

"I know what a typhoon is," he muttered.

Koizumi looked at me. "She's kidding."

"No," I said. "Mr. Tanaka said the same thing."

It still looked nice enough. We all looked around, held out our hands. But Ms. Zhu said, "Soon. I believe it."

Mr. Neils looked at us. "You know what that means?"

"No helicopters?" said Koizumi.

"Helicopter *ga nai*," said Mr. Neils. *"Sappari ga nai."*

"Then . . . what'll they *do*?" I said. They had to do *something*. I mean, there was just no way they couldn't do something.

"God fucking damnit," he said in English.

"I'm very sorry," said Ms. Zhu.

"Well, hell, it isn't your fault."

We went back inside. For a second I thought there was a fire, but it was just Mr. Tanaka smoking.

"Did she tell you?" was all he said. *Kanojou oshieta?* He'd always had a causal way of talking, for a teacher, but now more than ever.

Mr. Neils nodded. "A hard rain's a-gonna fall," he said in English. Then he muttered something in English that I didn't understand but that I guessed must have had to do with something in his own life: "Fuck you, Tom."

None of us said much. We went into the café, one of us following another, not really knowing what do—and Ms. Zhu just hovered around us, holding her hands to keep them from flapping. It must have been scary, all those guys standing there not saying anything. Then Mr. Neils went around behind the counter and opened the fridge. He started putting sandwiches on the counter, like a gambler laying out cards.

Mr. Tanaka stared at him.

"What are we supposed to do?" said Mr. Neils and shrugged. "We're at the goddamn mercy of those helicopters."

Helicopters that might or might not come now. Like angels from heaven.

I looked out the window and it couldn't have been more than fifteen minutes, but already everything had gone gray. The trees were rocking. Shadows raced up and down the walls.

"Come here and get your goddamn sandwich," said Mr. Neils.

Mr. Tanaka was pacing with his hands behind his back and didn't say anything.

"What about you kids? You hungry?"

Then the rain started to fall. It was like a switch flipped.

It was quieter inside, but you could still hear it: *bam, bam, bam,* hitting the roof. Hitting the windows. Hitting the ground outside. At first it came in waves, like somebody was splashing us with a hose, like special effects, and it hit the window and started to run down, then another wave. *Bam.* I thought about the houses with the tiles. People in Taiwan were used to this.

Mr. Neils went right to the windows and stood there, leaning forward, like he was daring somebody. Now *I* was scared of him; he'd moved so fast. It was hard to believe we had been sitting, talking, just half an hour ago.

"Are the door and windows closed?" he asked Ms. Zhu, and she looked terrified and nodded. "Fuck," he said quietly.

Then we heard something else outside.

It was the second thing none of us could believe. Me and Koizumi went and stuck ourselves to the glass, and Mr. Neils stood there with this *expression.* We looked out and there, where the rain was turning the dirt into mud that would suck a person down in a second—you could hardly see now through the rain— two cars had pulled up. White-and-black cars with some kind of writing on them.

"Who's got a raincoat?" said Mr. Neils. "Nobody?"—then he went for the door. He pushed through and went outside in just his cloth jacket, and right away I saw his hair plastered down and his pants stuck to his legs, and the wind came in and Ms. Zhu ran back, and Mr. Tanaka ran to force the door shut again and I helped him. Mr. Neils ran down the stairs to where the cars were, holding his arms over his head.

A bunch of guys got out of the cars all dressed in slickers. They were just the kind of raincoat you get out of a bag, transparent and yellow. Mr. Neils yelled at them and waved his arms, and I couldn't tell if he was excited or angry. One of them talked to Mr. Neils, and they all came back. We opened the door—the rain hit us in the face—and they all came in at once, and Mr. Neils threw his wet jacket on the floor with a swear, and one of the men put back the hood of his slicker.

He just looked calm. It was the detective, the funny old one from last night who had been eating a hard-boiled egg.

Mr. Tanaka took his cigarette out of his mouth.

"I'm sorry," he said in English. "I've forgotten your name."

"Detective Chao, Mr. Taka."

"Tanaka."

"Jesus," said Mr. Neils. "You guys are insane, driving in this shit."

"No helicopters," said Detective Chao, still looking calm. "No dogs." He looked skinny and old and there were spots on his head, but it was obvious that not even the rain could knock him down. Koizumi and I just stood there with our mouths open. "But," he said, "so you cannot say Taiwan cops are lazy, I brought you men."

"You guys are out of your fucking minds."

"So you cannot say I am lazy, I brought you six of my best

men," and they were all standing there. "It is very, very dangerous, but still we will look."

Mr. Tanaka looked angry. I thought he was going to explode.
But instead he bowed and said, "*Arigatou gozaimashita*. Thank
you . . . very much."

They were all dripping water on the floor. All of a sudden the
room was full of people. And then Mr. Pickett came in through a
side door, holding his head, saying, "Fu-uck, what all the hell is
this? It feels like fucking Keith Moon's banging on my head."

Mr. Neils looked at him and said, "Pickett." Then he looked
quickly around and said, "Where are the other two kids?"

It felt like somebody stuck a knife in me.

I try my best. I'm the Class Rep, and I try to do my best. I try
to look after everyone.

"I don't know," I said.

"*Wakarimasen?* What the hell is that *wakarimasen, nantte wakarimasen?*" Then he was right in my face and I stepped back, and
he said, "Sorry. Sorry. Does anybody know? Please tell me where
the other two kids are."

Detective Chao didn't look surprised by this.

Koizumi took off running, his shoes squeaking like crazy. A
moment later he came back, shaking his head.

"Sumiregawa's not there."

"Kamakiri?"

"No. No."

"Well," said Mr. Neils, in a very flat, hard voice, "I suggest
we go and fucking find them."

We started running in every direction.

"Sumiregawa!"

"Kamakiri!"

"Ponytail!"

"Michiko-*san*, say something!"

"Seiji-*kun*!"

I ran into Mr. Pickett by the back door. He was looking out, out where the rain had gotten thicker than ever. I looked at him and he shook his head. Two of the policemen went by, still wearing their wet slickers. Koizumi ran up. I knew from looking at him that he knew I was about to cry.

"Class Rep. It's not your fault. . . ." He was gasping for air. "I—I didn't think of it, either."

I just looked at him.

Why did I feel like all this was happening to *me*?

Everything happens for a reason. It's all part of the beautiful story God is trying to tell. You just have to figure out what you're supposed to learn. I guess this was happening to everyone, and everyone was supposed to learn something—but like hell *I* could figure out what it was!

MICHIKO KAMAKIRI

Maybe **it's** time to admit I just don't get anything anymore.

I mean, you can make lists and write down all the things you want. Then something really happens and it's just like—*like*.

Koizumi. I mean, I had never thought about him before. Except that he was nice and liked helping people. And he was Class Rep's friend, so back when I thought *maybe* I had a chance with Class Rep, I thought I could, you know, get to know *him* and . . . Well, you have to look at all your options.

And then when Class Rep told me, I only thought about him a little. I wondered. I dreamed. But then *it* happened, and from right when I woke up the next morning, all tied up in my stupid sleeping bag, I couldn't stop thinking about him for one second. How strong he was but how gently he held me. That silly grin and how it cut up his cute little face. And how brave he'd been, like a knight, to come by and just knock on my door . . . !

Maybe in the end I took the initiative, but it was still really brave of him. And the way he came out and *said*, "I blew my fuse." It made me laugh every time I thought about it, but at the same time I felt like a million degrees inside.

I was totally, madly, crazily in love with Koizumi, Koizumi, and Ponytail and Class Rep and even Jun Matsumoto and those guys from SMAP might have been another species.

Maybe there is no such thing as true love. Or maybe when you're in love, it really is true love, but a big part of it is that *they* love *you*. But then, how do they . . . ?

I totally don't get it at all.

But there was no way I could even look him in the face for a few days. I just wanted to dig a hole somewhere and sit in it and, like, *think* about him.

So when I got up, instead of knocking on their door, I just walked around in circles with my knees close together. I didn't remember that I had been so scared before I fell asleep. What was there to be scared of? We'd find Kari, Mai, and Taeko out in the woods and yell at them for about a whole day for making us worry so much; then we could all go home and Class Rep could go out with Kari and Sumiregawa could go out with Chizu Sato and Jin-*kun* could go out with Sakura and we could all have one big quadruple date.

Senior trip *banzai*! Happy endings forever.

I went upstairs, where Mr. Tanaka was sleeping—he totally sawed logs—and I even went outside. It felt like it was going to be a nice day, not windy at all. Finally I cooled down a bit. I would have to act normal because I knew not everyone was as happy and totally in love with a wonderful guy who loved them back. They didn't have the secret knowledge that everything had to turn out alright.

Then I was walking down the hall and I heard, around the corner, the door of the guys' room opening. Then I heard Koizumi and Class Rep talking. Not talking about *me*, thank God, but I stayed right where I was, flat against the wall. Then I heard them walking off and I waited until I couldn't hear them anymore.

I peeked around the corner. I don't know, I felt like they might come back. Instead, a minute later, Sumiregawa came out.

He had already tied back his hair, and he put his arms up and yawned. He was in his undershirt.

Amazing, I thought; he so isn't as cute as I thought he was. He just looked nice, and sleepy, and I wanted to talk to him.

"*Ohaa*, Mii-*chan*," he said, supercasual.

"*Ohayou!* Seiji-*kun*."

"You look happy."

"I don't know. Do I?"

"In point of fact you look ecstatic."

"Hey, I don't know words like that. Use smaller words."

"The story of my life," said Sumiregawa. He went back into the room. I thought he was going back to sleep, but a second later he came out with his school coat on—but unbuttoned. "I guess we're going to see a helicopter today," he said.

"That would be cool."

"I think everyone is in a good mood. The helicopters will only assist matters."

"I hope they find them."

"Well, that goes without saying.—I always take a walk in the morning. It's good for your health. Want to join me?"

Wow. No *ba-dump* at all.

"What are you," I said, "an old man?"

"*Kokoro wa furui,*" he said. The heart is old.

"How do you even find time to walk before school? It starts at like seven in the morning."

"'Early to bed and early to rise makes a man healthy, wealthy, and wise.' Benjamin Franklin said that. It rhymes in English."

"Benjamin Franklin?"

"The Founding Father. He didn't *really* discover electricity, though. Are you coming or what?"

"Oh, sure."

"Let's go out the back. I'm pretty sure I heard our friends going the other way, and I like a *bit* of company, but four's a crowd."

How did he know? I felt the exact same way.

Walking shoulder to shoulder with a boy. Talking about intelligent things. Now that I didn't feel like I *had* to be intelligent, I sort of felt more like I could be.

When we got outside, the first thing Sumiregawa did was take out a pack of Seven Stars cigarettes and some matches. I was really surprised.

"Our little secret, okay?" he said and winked at me.

"Um—okay."

"You don't mind, do you?"

"Um—no, no."

Actually, I don't like the smell of cigarettes, but I knew he hadn't smoked in a while, so he probably needed it.

"Mr. Tanaka's been smoking like it's burnable trash day. I don't think he'd mind."

Sumiregawa laughed. "I don't see how they expect everyone to quit smoking just because it kills you," he said as he lit up and inhaled. "It betrays a lack of the existential perspective on their part."

"The existential—huh?"

"Bluntly stated, that everybody dies," he said and started puffing. "If they just made being alive less searingly painful, maybe people would quit. As for me, when they take out my throat, I'll be smoking through the hole in that little box they put in."

I laughed. Yeah, it was better like this. It was better to have a friend who made jokes like that. A boyfriend to be nice and hold you.

"A cigarette is like a comma in life," he said. "It breaks up periods of time. If you're not a *chain* smoker, you just smoke whenever something *happens*. It's a way of marking it."

But I didn't really want to talk about how he was killing himself.

"Hey," I said, "d'you miss Chizu?"

He raised his eyebrows. "What do you mean?"

"I mean like, she confessed her love, didn't she?"

All of a sudden Sumiregawa looked really embarrassed.

We'd gone a little way down the path. He looked back at the building—there was no one there—then he leaned toward me and said, "This will be our little secret, too, okay?"

Eagerly I nodded.

He leaned even closer and whispered it in my ear.

I jumped back. "No way! Like *shounen ai*?"

"Actually," he said, and he made a face, "my life has very little in common with a 'boys' love' comic book. But yes, roughly."

"Sorry. But really, seriously?"

"Really seriously."

"Poor Chizu," I said. "But did you tell her?"

"I didn't have the heart," he said, and he poured smoke out of his mouth—away from me, which was nice of him.

The air was really still. The smoke just hung there, in coils like snakes, then slithered away in every direction.

"So what's the use?" he said like he was quoting again. *"See the smoke float free . . . Into ever-colder coldness. It's the same with me."*

"Who's that?"

"Some Westerner.—Anyway, I'm serious; don't tell anyone. Nobody knows yet."

"Not even Class Rep? But you were sleeping in his room!"

"I'll tell him eventually. I'm sure he'll understand, but—I'm not ready yet."

We walked a little farther.

"Oh, wow," I said.

There was the gorge. But it was totally different from yesterday.

There hadn't been that many people around, but still, when it was just the two of us—it was so big and empty. *Empty*, that was weird. It's hard to think of something being *really* empty, and not like full of air, but that was what it was. Just us and the rocks and the water.

The cliff on the other side stood there, and now it wasn't pretty scenery, it was something giant that stood there not caring about us.

"It feels like we're the last two people on earth," I said.

"Kind of spooky, isn't it?"

"Yeah, but—exciting, too."

"I know what you mean."

We walked out on the road. It was damp from the dew over-night, and there were some big bugs—I saw a praying mantis—sunning themselves.

"Too bad Hirata isn't here," I said. I felt really bad that I said he raped Taeko-*chan*. There was really no way, was there, but when I said it, I was really mad. "Hey, look at that butterfly! It's as big as my head, don't you think?—You're not looking."

Sumiregawa had gone up to the railing. He was looking down, the cigarette hanging on his lip. He had already smoked to the filter, and in a second he spit it out and watched it fall.

"It's a long way down."

"A long way, yeah."

I was kind of glad that he couldn't describe it any better than I could. No fancy words could stick to it, I felt, only simple words. *Big. Long. Empty.*

The river was fast and flat. The rocks on either side were totally white—just like where it had been the last time I saw Kari.

"'Man is a thinking reed,'" said Sumiregawa.

"What does that mean?"

"Never mind."

Reed just made me think of Ganryu, the big swordsman who had fought Musashi; that was what his name meant. Maybe I wasn't so smart after all.

We went a little farther.

"We'd better not get too far," I said, but I didn't mean it. It felt so good to walk.

"We'll stay on the road. Let's go down to the temple. They should be doing their morning chanting right about now."

We both looked at our watches: it was eight-fifty-five. He lit another cigarette and we started walking.

"Seiji-*kun*," I said, "why'd you stay?"

"Class Rep called me his lieutenant. I couldn't very well back out after that."

"'Lieutenant,' heh.— But is that all?"

"Well . . ." He rolled the cigarette in his lips. "I guess I kind of felt bad for Class Rep. I mean, obviously we all do. But it seemed to me like he was setting himself up for a big disappointment. You know what I mean? And that when it happened, someone like me should be there with him. What about you—why did you stay?"

I told him the truth: "I just didn't want to see those guys ever again."

"I can see why you would feel that way." He nodded. "What about now?"

"I don't know." I was squinting and fidgeting in the morning sun. "It's all really weird. I feel like when I go back, everything's gonna be different."

"Me, too."

"Like time is different here . . . time and space. Sorry. That sounds like something *you'd* say. Did I steal your line?"

He laughed. "Maybe."

Then he said, "Nobody really understands what's going on here."

"What, you mean *you* do?"

"No." He shook his head. "Not a bit."

Then we could see the temple. There was the bridge, like yesterday; a suspension bridge, like a miniature Golden Gate. On the other side was the building, the gold statue of Amida Buddha and the tower that Sakura had leaned off while Jin-*kun* had yelled at her to be careful.

His voice dropped as he said, "Listen. You can hear them from here."

And sure enough, I heard it. Now, *there* was something spooky. They were chanting words of just one syllable, and in like a flat rhythm, one after another. And their voices sounded the same, but then one voice would rise up for a second and one word would just hang there. I don't know Chinese, but I recognized one word: *kong*. The Chinese reading of the character for *empty*. Or *sky*. And *kong* rose up like with extra feeling—only there *was* no feeling—and hung there.

And there was a sound like a drum, or like someone hitting a board, but it *echoed* in just this weird way I can't describe.

"What's that?" I whispered. "That *tok*?"

"A wooden fish," said Sumiregawa.

"What's a wooden fish?"

"Just a musical instrument."

"I don't like this," I said. "Let's go."

And then I jumped because the chanting got louder like they'd heard us, but I guess they were just getting

jie di jie di bo ro jie di bo ro jie di

to the end.

"Had enough already?" said Sumiregawa. He laughed and

threw his second cigarette in the river. I thought the way he laughed was kind of mean. We kept walking, and when the sound of the chanting faded out, I was glad.

"The Heart Sutra," he said.

"You understood that?"

"Enough of the words. I have a recording of Tibetan monks chanting it that sends chills up your spine."

That sent plenty of chills up my spine, thanks, I thought.

"You sure know a lot."

He shrugged. "You pick these things up."

"I can't believe you're only in junior high."

"It's not really anything."

"Seiji-*kun*," I said as we followed the bending road, "yesterday you said something about something being, like, a corruption of real Buddhism. What does that mean?"

He'd been superembarrassed by me flattering him, I could tell, and he was glad to talk about that.

"It applies equally to Japan," he said. "But the thing is . . . most religions, as I see it, are about explaining things to people. They all start with a creation myth and go from there. But Buddhism— pure Buddhism—isn't about that at all. It's about the ultimate incomprehensibility of everything."

"What about the Pure Land and stuff?"

"Just a bunch of myths. That's what I mean about the corruption."

The bad thing about talking with a smart person is, you never know if another smart person might be able to argue against what they're saying, even if you do kind of understand. All you can do is nod.

"'Subhuti,'" he quoted from somewhere, "'what does your mind say? Form is emptiness and emptiness form. Large bodies are not large bodies, therefore they are large bodies.'"

"Uh-huh."

"In theory it isn't nihilistic because if there is no self, then the self is everything and everything is the self. But I don't know if I buy that. I think I'd rather have an explanation. But if the explanation is false, you have to throw it out."

To be honest, it was really getting beyond me. I started thinking about Koizumi and the way his hands had felt behind my back.

"Hey, Seiji-*kun*," I said, "you ever kissed a boy?"

He blinked. "Well—no."

"Not even like on a dare?"

"No."

"You should get a boyfriend," I said. "It's fun."

Then I looked over his shoulder and started screaming my head off.

It was all because of that stupid chant and the way Sumiregawa had laughed. But even if not for that, I would have screamed because it was the most horrible thing possible.

Standing there at the edge of the road was a real ghost. It was Mai Mori, and she was all white and puffy and her eyes were shining, and there were cuts all over her, and her mouth was open, and oh God I don't want to *think* about it because it's happening all over again and there she was, dead, in front of us.

Sumiregawa spun around. He screamed. I was behind him,

JACOB RITARI   153

but all of a sudden he was so skinny, and if he hadn't grabbed my arm I seriously think I would have run and thrown myself over the cliff.

"*Stay back!*" he screamed. "*Just don't come any closer! Don't! Don't!*"

I started making the sign of the cross over myself, like I had seen people do. Just anything, anything that would help. Oh, God.

She just stood there. The expression on her face, it was like she couldn't imagine anything wrong. She must have looked like that when she died.

And then she *said* something.

"What're y'all scared of?"

Sumiregawa's grip on my arm hurt.

"You," he said.

She stared at us with those (God) drowned eyes.

"Why?"

"*Yurei,*" I said. "You're a ghost."

She looked at her hands. Her white, puffy, scraped hands. There was dried blood all *over* her.

"I'm not a ghost," she said.

"Go away," said Sumiregawa. "Just go away!"

"But I'm not a ghost. Why'd you say that?"

Her voice was kind of hoarse . . . but she sounded like Mai. Small and tiny and sweet, her dumb accent.

Then it was almost funny because Sumiregawa swallowed and said, "Prove it."

She brought up her hand. Dirt. Cuts on it. The hand of a ghost.

"Touch me," she said.

Sumiregawa shook his head.

Because he knew as well as I did that, forget Buddhism, forget God and boyfriends, everything, if you touched a ghost something awful would happen.

"I'm not a ghost." And then she looked really sad. "Touch me."

Very, very slowly, Sumiregawa brought up his hand. And he reached out. I let go of him; I stepped back. I was ready to run, even though I knew it wouldn't do any good. . . .

Sumiregawa put his fingers between hers. I saw him shudder. But his hand didn't go through hers and his eyes didn't pop out of his head and he didn't start rotting. He stared at his hand and I stared at their hands.

Mai smiled. "You see?"

And then I screamed again because it was even worse this way.

"Who are you?" said Sumiregawa.

She looked at him funny. "Mai-*chan*," she said.

"Who am I?"

"Seiji-*kun—deshou?*"

"Oh my God," he said. "Oh my God."

He let go of her hand and she collapsed, fell right down on the road, and it was obvious now she really wasn't a ghost. When she hit the ground, her fragile body jumped like it was made out of sticks.

"Seiji-*kun!*" I said.

Somehow he knew what I meant, and he grabbed my arm again. It hurt again, but it was still good, good.

"It's really her," I said.

"Oh, my God. Look at her. What happened?"

Her blouse was torn open. Her skin was white and sticky just like a dead person's. And there were cuts all over her.

"Is she dead?" I asked suddenly. "Is she dead?"

He knelt down, and now I knew he was just as brave as anyone. He lifted her hand and took her pulse. Then he shook his head. "We've got to get her back. I don't know how long she'll make it."

A part of me (God) wanted to say, crazily: Oh, let's just leave her here. Pretend we never saw anything. Please.

"Yeah," I said. "But I'm not touching her."

"I know, but you've got to."

"I'm not touching her!"

"Fine," he said.

I couldn't believe it. He hoisted her up on his back, her head rolling around, her drowned-girl's hair all over his shoulder. Her skinny white arms around his skinny neck. I knew I was seeing something amazing. He really was really, really brave.

"Seiji-*kun* . . ."

"Shit," he said. "I'll never make it."

Then it started to rain.

PETER NEILS

Ten minutes after we'd noticed they were gone, with all of us pacing around and getting cabin fever in there, ready to pounce on each other, I saw them through the rain-slicked windows where I had been standing thinking what the hell was I going to do. I yelled for Detective Chao.

They came out of the trees in the downpour, looking like they were about to drown standing up. Between them they were carrying a tiny female corpse.

"Jesus fucking Christ," I said.

Chao rubbed his hands together.

"Ah," he said. "Now things get more interesting."

What an unfeeling asshole he was.

I didn't like the detective, and he didn't like me. He seemed to think I was an upstart—a judgment that, with prematurely graying hair, I am not used to getting—and I thought he was a complacent old bastard who pretended to some worldly wisdom. He thought he deserved a medal for showing up in that storm, and he'd said to me, "Do you know how many children go missing every day? But when it's someone from a developed country, like America, like Japan, it turns into a circus. People in many parts of the world are quite used to the fact."

"You think *I* don't know that?" I said.

It was a reason to be *more* upset, not less. How many weeks, I wanted to ask, did *you* spend in Sierra Leone during the most brutal civil war the country had ever seen? How many children did *you* know to go missing without a word of explanation?

But this is all beside the point.

The shorter Japanese kid, Koizumi, yelled, "Incoming!"

He grabbed one half of the double doors and I grabbed the other, and when our friends made the porch, we hauled it open and they fell inside. One big wet heap on the floor; there was no telling the living from the dead. And right away there was a bad wet smell.

Koizumi threw himself on the pile and pulled one girl loose. Through her plastered hair, I recognized the girl who had been with us last night, Michiko. He seemed fond of her because he held her very tightly and said how worried he'd been.

The boy, Sumiregawa, got to his feet. He had a ponytail that, wet, looked like a snake slithering over his shoulder, and big sensitive eyes.

He walked up to the boy named Tohru and said, "Sorry, Class Rep."

Tohru embraced him. Meanwhile, Pickett and I were struggling to get the door shut. The wind had picked up and now was dead set on getting inside.

"It's a miracle," Tohru was saying as he held his friend. *Kiseki da.*

It's funny, having to translate for yourself out of another language. It makes you think about words that have been so used in English that they've lost all meaning. I was so used to hearing *kiseki* in a religious context, referring to things like people disappearing into the Pure Land, that I actually thought—well, was it a miracle? Or was it a miracle of another order that a typhoon had chosen that moment to hit us?

Detective Chao was leaning over what I thought of instinctively as the dead girl. There was no way she could be alive; I had only seen so many cuts on the bodies of street-fight victims. But then why had they gone to the insane trouble of hauling her back here?

"She's alive," said Chao. Then he looked up at Tanaka, who was standing there clutching his arms. "She is one of yours?"

Tanaka nodded.

The other girl, still being held in a death grip by Koizumi, tried to speak, although her teeth were chattering. "She's n-not a ghost. She's real."

"I can see that," I said.

"The others?" said Tohru, moving forward. "The others?"

Sumiregawa shook his head.

We were all clustered around the doors. There was so much tension there, so much anguished energy, that we were bound to fly apart. The girl took off running without explanation, and Koizumi ran after her. Just to be safe, I suppose, one of Chao's men ran after them. Mr. Tanaka started pacing off quickly, rubbing the gooseflesh on his arms. Tohru walked off, and Sumiregawa followed him. That left only me, Pickett, and the detective and his nameless men, like some honor guard in the uniforms of their yellow raincoats.

"Her hold on life is like a drowner with one finger on the shore," said Chao, calm as ever. "Who here knows medicine?"

Apparently none of his men did. I started to say that I had picked up something, but then Pickett said, "I do."

I looked at him. "What?"

"I was an EMT two years at fucking St. Francis of Assisi," he said.

"Man, you had better not be shitting me."

"Why the fuck would I lie about something like that? Get this girl up on a table."

So two of the men lifted her, arms and legs hanging like rope, and trouped at Pickett's direction out of the room. Before he left he turned to the others: "I want hot water. I want towels. I want—shit, what do I want? Any first-aid crap you can find, I know they got some. . . ."

It was unlikely the cops knew much English, but they made out the crucial words and went into motion immediately, professionals.

"I'm sorry," I said. "I'm sure you know your shit."

But some of the force had gone out of him. "Well," he said, looking as pale as the rest of us, "Jesus. It's been a while."

It wouldn't be right to say that I prayed. But growing up Catholic, you can never fully get it out of your system. Mechanically, only to calm my own mind, if you like, I recited the words to myself: *Hail Mary, full of Grace. The Lord is with thee. Blessed are thee among women, and blessed is the fruit of your womb, Jesus.*

Holy Mary, mother of God, pray for us sinners, now and at the hour of our deaths. Amen.

I had always liked the sound of it. It did calm me down, and briefly I felt like maybe things would be alright. Of course it didn't last, but it was like smoking a cigarette.

When I find myself in times of trouble, Mother Mary comes to me. . . .

Now and at the hour of our deaths. I once had a conversation with Chris Hitchens. He told me that religion preyed on people's fear of death, and I told him that if not for religion —it seemed to me—a lot of people might get away with never thinking about death.

I paced around in the hall like an expectant father, though my own days of fatherhood were so far behind me I couldn't remember if it actually felt like this. Tanaka was sitting on a folding chair. Given the choice between smoking and being in any kind of proximity to the sick girl, he had eventually chosen this.

"Aren't you glad?" I asked him.

"Not yet," he said.

I looked at him, sweat glossing his dark forehead. Trying to read the mask of his face—and Tanaka took that Asian stoicism to new heights. But I could make out something. Surely it had to be . . . his jaw was clenched, his eyes locked, but at that moment he wanted desperately to talk to another human being.

Standing behind him, I said quietly, not looking at him, "Y'know I meant to ask from before. How'd your English get so good? I mean, I've been in Japan; most businessmen can't talk like that."

He shook his head. "I did college in the States. Two years. In the end I couldn't keep up, I went back."

"Why?"

Not sure what I was asking him—why he'd gone or why he'd left—he shrugged. "I wanted to play basketball. But it was all stupid." Looking up at the ceiling, the stuttering lights, he said, "Why go somewhere else? It's stupid. What you're looking for, if you can't find it at home, where are you going to find it?"

"I guess that's pretty much my experience."

But giving up means that at least things can't get any worse. The prayer of the disillusioned traveler: let there be no surprises, good or bad.

"You might as well stay home," he said.

"But even then, would you be safe?"

"Hmm."

They were in there for about a half hour, Pickett and two of the policeman who had some first-aid training. Finally Pickett came out, his face and bald head shiny with sweat, and leaned on the wall, and I think he can be forgiven his moment of melodrama when he said, "She's going to live. That goddamn beautiful girl is going to live."

I embraced him. "You are the fucking man."

"I'd forgot how good it felt," he said, "working like that. Right on the fucking *edge* of it, man."

Tanaka stood up. "Is she awake?"

"Umm," said Pickett, "yeah, she is. But . . ."

One of the policemen came out, shaking his head. He had

taken off his raincoat and was in plainclothes. He'd rolled up his sleeves—and though he'd washed his hands, they still had a tell-tale red cast. He looked at me and tapped the side of his head.

"What?"

"I wouldn't go talk to her right now," said Pickett.

But Tanaka went in.

"Don't say I didn't warn you, man!"

A moment later he came back out, as white as a sheet.

"Is it bad?" I asked, stupidly.

He didn't say anything.

Detective Chao opened up a new carton of Paradise cigarettes—which he'd somehow kept dry under his raincoat—tamped the bottom with his hand, and pulled out the cigarette that stuck out the furthest. This he turned upside down and reinserted into the pack.

I don't know what meaning the ritual had for him. As far as I know, that cigarette, the "lucky" one, is reserved for postcoital purposes, but I doubt that was what the detective had in mind. He pulled out another cigarette, lit it with a plastic Bic, and took three pulls on it. Then he took out a notepad and placed it on the table in front of him.

We were sitting around a table in the cafeteria—the detective, myself, Tanaka, Tohru, and the policemen. The other two boys and the girl had gone off somewhere, probably to dry off, and Pickett was lying down, maybe hoping to sleep off his heroism. The parks lady, Ms. Zhu, seemed to have vanished. Outside, the rain kept falling and the wind blew. We were in the darkness of the storm, and three lanterns had been placed in the room, making it seem conspiratorial. Or as if we were telling ghost stories.

Chao started to speak: "The girl has had what I believe you call a breakdown. The mental function is compromised. Still, I think it best—and I do not think anyone will disagree with me—that we try to get as much of her story as possible before we try a search in these, hmm, inclement conditions."

His diction was flawless, but he had a funny way of pronouncing certain words. In*clement.*

A haze of smoke hung around the ceiling. Tanaka and I had already smoked one each.

"One of my men, Li," he indicated the officer, who nodded, "who is good with children, tried to speak with her. He did not have luck. However, it is the story of those children who claim to have found her—" That seemed like a weird way of putting it, I thought; were they lying?—"that she spoke with them and seemed to know about herself. Then it is my theory that she will respond in different ways to different people—which is as much to say that one of us might have more luck. Then I propose that we speak to her individually and see what we can find out. We all agree?"

It was clear from his tone that he would brook no argument, so I nodded. No one else said anything. He had probably been talking to me for the most part anyway, since I was the only one who seemed like I might think I knew better than him.

"Now . . ." His eyes scanned us one by one. His head turned like some ancient piece of machinery.

"Mr. Neils," he said, "claims to be"—again with the *claims*;

did he just not know what that meant?—"a journalist. Then we can assume that he has experience talking with people and getting answers. What do you think of this . . . Mr. Neils?"

I wasn't sure what he was getting at.

"If you want me to do it, I'll do it," I said.

His eyes moved past me.

"On the other hand," he went on, "Mr. Tanaka and young Tohru were both acquainted with the girl before, as were the boy and girl who found her. It is possible that she would respond to them better."

"I can do it," said Tohru. *Boku wa dekimasu.*

He was sitting next to me.

I put my hand on his arm. "Are you sure about that?" I said to him in Japanese. "Maybe you should let your teacher handle this one."

Tanaka bit his thumbnail.

"You look like you don't think that's such a hot idea."

I hadn't seen the girl yet, and he hadn't told me what he had seen.

"Since Mr. Chao knows so much," he said, "why doesn't he tell us what to do?"

My eyes snapped to Chao. He didn't react at all. Slowly, exhaling smoke, he looked at the empty space between me and Tanaka.

"Mr. Taka. Is there anything you would like to say?"

Now I watched Tanaka carefully. The last thing we needed was these two getting at each other's throats, and it seemed like for some reason, the detective had it in for him. But Tanaka only rolled his jaw and said, "Nothing."

"Are you sure? Now is your chance if you want to complain about the way I do things."

What the hell was this? I thought, but I didn't say anything. Both of them wanted to get those girls back more than anything, because it was their jobs, if nothing else. Whatever beef they had—maybe it had something to do with their nationalities— couldn't they put it aside for now? I mean, Jesus Christ.

Without looking at the detective, just as the detective wasn't looking at him, Tanaka said, "I appreciate that you came out here. You know how to do your job. So why don't you just tell us what you want to do?"

I looked back at Chao—I thought that had been pretty re-strained. But the detective blew out a cone of smoke and said, "Why not . . . ? Mr. Tanaka. You do not sound as if you'd like to be told what to do. You expect to go to another country and have everything work the way you're used to?"

"That's the opposite of what I said."

"Perhaps you think every country should do things the way you do in Japan?"

They still weren't looking at each other. The cops were ex-pressionless; Tohru just looked confused—maybe he couldn't follow the English. I braced myself, locking my hands together under the table, but then Tanaka got up suddenly. Without a word, slowly, he walked out of the room through the open door.

I shut my eyes with relief; that could have been worse. They were grown men, and they would work it out. I didn't say any-thing, even when Tohru looked at me, and the detective went on like nothing had happened: "Of course I could try myself. . . ."

He sounded like he knew, too, that it wasn't a good idea. There was a silence.

"Tohru-*kun*?" I said. "Can I talk to you outside for a second?"

He nodded. *"H-hai."*

We got up and left the room, everyone staying quiet right where they were. The only noise the rain.

Outside in the hall, with Tanaka's still unmade bed—no sign of him; I guessed he'd gone off to cool down—Tohru sat on the floor. I stood next to him with my arm on the wall.

"You want to talk to me . . . ?"

"Yeah. I'm going to talk a little in English because it's more natural to me," I said. "Just give a yell if you're not following, okay?"

He nodded.

"Now," I said, "you're the Class Representative, I understand. Is that right?"

"Hai."

"I understand that's a pretty big deal. Is that why you stayed?"

"Hai."

"Because you feel that you're responsible for everyone."

He nodded.

"Well . . . like I said before, I think you're a really brave kid. All four of you. But the thing is . . . there's only so much one human being can do."

"I don't understand," he said.

"You don't understand my English, or you just don't get what I mean?"

He hesitated. "The second."

He was looking up at me. A handsome kid with mature, calm eyes.

"Tohru," I said, "whatever is in that room, it gave your teacher a scare. Now, he looks to me like a pretty tough guy, am I right?"

"Tough?" he said. "Hah. Yeah."

"Now, I haven't been in there myself, so I don't know what it was. I can't say anything for sure. But what I suspect is that if you do this, then for the rest of your life it will be an albatross around your neck. Sorry, you wouldn't get that. It will be a big, big weight on your soul.

"Now, I've seen things I wish I could forget. And once you've seen something, you can't ever *un*see it. And that's what I mean when I say that it will be a weight for you. Because you won't be able to forget it for the rest of your life . . . and that's a long time."

"Nierusu-*san*," he said.

"Yeah?"

He smiled and said in as fair an echo of me as he could manage, "I'm going to speak in Japanese because it's more natural for me. Just give me a yell if you're not following . . . okay?"

"Uh-huh."

He breathed in and said, "*Boku wa iinchou da. San nen kara kono kurasu no iinchou. Minna itsumo mamote shinakucha. Zutto, zutto mamote shitain kedosa. Dareka mamote shinakucha kara, boku nanda. Mamote shinakereba, boku wa iranai desu. Sappari iranai—gomi mitai dayo.*

"Boku wa shounen dake. Ima 'iinchou dake' to ieru dake-dosa . . . ima dekinakereba, mirai ni zen-zen dekinai ze. Wakaru kai?"

I'm the Class Representative. For three years I've been representative for this class. I always have to protect everyone. I wish I could protect everyone forever. Somebody's got to do it, so that person is me. If I can't protect them, I'm useless. Totally useless—like garbage.

I'm just a kid. You want to say, "You're just a Class Representative" . . . but if I can't do it now, then in the future I'll never, ever be able to do it. You understand?

"I think you're making a big mistake," I said.

But I had told him everything I had to say, and he had told me everything he had to say.

TOHRU MARUYAMA

want to tell what happened. I don't want to talk about how I felt, only what I saw.

I went into the room. It was about as big as my bedroom at home; I mean, you could just fit a bed inside. There were no windows. There was one light on the ceiling, just a lightbulb, and it was on. The room was full of filing cabinets and there was a metal table in the middle, the kind that folds up. The table was clean, and they must have done something to Mai on it, but they'd cleaned up the room since then. She was sitting there on the table.

They had taken off her clothes, and I don't know if they had given her a bath or what, but they had cleaned her up a little. Now she was wearing a white T-shirt that was a little big for her and red swimming trunks. The T-shirt said, *Drive away with me. Lot's run away together.* Later they would tell me they'd gotten the clothes out of the lost and found—I guess nobody had a change because our clothes were all back at the hotel. Mai's hair was clean, not clinging all over her face like when they'd carried her in. They had cleaned the dirt off her face and arms. They had washed the cuts, so there were just red lines, and they had put one bandage on her forehead and one on her left arm. There was already a little blood on the one on her arm. They must have gotten the bandages from a first-aid kit.

I don't know what was wrong with her when they brought her in. They said she was really bad, but I don't know if it was from losing blood. Maybe it was shock—whatever that means; it's just what they say in dramas.

She was sitting forward a little. Like I said, her hair wasn't in her face, but it was hanging around it. She didn't look up when I came in. Her hands were in her lap, and she was looking down at them. Her palms were all cut up, and there were two big, square bandages on them.

There was another chair. My hands were shaking a little, but I pulled it up and sat down across from her. I put my arms on the table.

"Mai-*chan*?"

"*Ohayou*, Class Rep," she said.

Her voice was really tiny. But not like she was scared—like she was daydreaming. She used to do that a lot. *Boh*, they called her. Spacey.

"Hey, you're a little mixed up," I said. I held out my watch, although she didn't look at it. "It's one-thirty. *Ohayou ja nakute— konnichiwa, ne?*"

She looked up at me. Her face was all swollen. There were cuts and scrapes on her cheeks. Also she still looked white, but *dark* underneath, like ice on a river. This is as close as I'm going to get to talking about how I felt: she looked just like I imagined a dead person would look.

But her eyes were bright. I didn't know if that was good.

"Mai-*chan*," I said, real slow, "what's my name?"

"Class Rep."

"I know, but what's my *real* name?"

"Class Rep."

"My name is Tohru. Tohru Ma-ru-ya-ma. Mai-*chan*, do you know where we are?"

She shook her head. It looked like she was smiling, but maybe her face was just stuck that way.

"Mai-*chan*, what's your name?"

"Mai-*chan*."

Then she laughed. It was a tinkly little sound, like a key falling down a well. Or like a piano key that isn't in tune.

"But what's your *family* name?"

It looked like she thought about it. Then she said, "Mai-*chan*."

"Mai, your family name is Mori. Mori."

"Mori?"

"That's right."

"Mai-*chan*," she said.

I sat back.

"Mori," I said really slowly. "Do you remember what I just said?"

She didn't say anything.

"What's your last name?"

"*Shiranu*," she said. Dunno.

But it was a word she hadn't said before.

"Mori, do you know where we are?" Then when she didn't answer, I asked again, "Mai-*chan*, do you know where we are?"

"*Shiranu.*"

"We're at Taroko Gorge," I said. "Ta-ro-ko."

"Ta-ro-ko."

"We were here on a class trip."

"Class trip."

"Mai-*chan*, do you remember Kari?"

"*Shiranu.*"

"Hi-ka-ri Hi-ra-o-ka? Or Taeko—Taeko Maeda?"

"*Shiranu.*"

"Kari was your friend," I said. "Who am I?"

"Class Rep."

"But what's my name?"

"Tohru Ma-ru-ya-ma," she said.

I swallowed and leaned forward again.

"Where are we?"

"Ta-ro-ko."

I raised my hand like I was going to touch her, but I pulled it back.

"That's right! You got it!"

"I got it?" she said. "That's swell."

Those funny country words she used.

"Mai-*chan*, can you tell me everything I just told you?"

"Mori Mai-*chan*. Tohru Ma-ru-ya-ma. Ta-ro-ko. Hi-ka-ri Hi-ra-o-ka."

"And who is Kari?"

"Kari's my friend."

"But don't you remember her? I mean, do you remember what she looks like?"

Then all of a sudden she started shaking. I fell back, but I caught myself on the edge of the table. It was like she was having a seizure or something. I should have gotten up, but I couldn't, and I couldn't call for anyone, either. But after a minute she calmed down. She ran her hands along both her arms, and then she didn't move. I wondered if I should get someone and tell them, stop the whole thing, but I didn't.

"Are you alright?"

Her eyes moved from side to side.

"I asked you about Kari. And Taeko."

"*Shiranu.*"

"Don't you know who they are? Who did I say they are?"

"My friends."

"But you don't know *about* them."

She shook her head.

"Do you remember what Kari looks like?"

"Yellow," she said.

Kari had a yellow hair band.

"That's right," I said. "Good job."

"Good job."

"Mai-*chan*," I leaned closer, "do you remember what happened?"

For a long time she looked at me. I kept being sure she was going to say something, so I didn't ask another question, but she didn't. So finally I asked, "Mai-*chan*, do you know where Kari is?"

"In the water," she said.

I bit my lip really hard. For a whole minute I was quiet, and she just looked at me.

"What's wrong, Class Rep?"

It was the first time she had asked a question.

"Nothing's wrong," I said, although I had a little trouble speaking. "Mai-*chan*, do you mean the river?"

"What river?"

"The river here. Do you mean Kari—do you mean she's in the river here, at Taroko?"

She shook her head.

"Where's Taeko?"

"*Shiranu.*"

"Where is the water? What water do you mean?"

"*Shiranu.*" Then she said something that really surprised me: "Sorry, Class Rep."

"'Sorry.' What for?"

"I'm not too good at answering questions. I'm not too smart."

"You're doing great," I said. "If you could just tell me where the water is."

She pointed. I don't know if she had any idea what she was pointing at.

"Mai-*chan*, did Kari—fall in the water?"

"*Shiranu.*"

"Mai. Did someone push Kari into the water?"

She didn't say anything.

Then she said, "Pikketto-*san*."

"Mai, what was that?"

"I remember . . . Pikketto-*san*."

"Mai, say that one more time. Please."

"I remember Pikketto-*san*. *Time* magazine." *Taimu magajin.* "*Sayonara*, Pikketto-*san*," she said. "*Sarabai.*"

Then she laughed again.

"Mai, this is very important," I said. "Does Pikketto-*san* have anything to do with Kari?"

"Kari?"

"Yes."

"*Shiranu. Shiranu yo.*"

"Mai, please—please."

Then she started to sing: "*Hoppara gatta sekai . . .*"

"Mai, please. *Onegaishimasu.*"

Hikuri kaeshi . . .

Hai, sarabai!

Hai, sarabai!

Hai, sarabai!

When she reached there, she stopped.

"Please," I said, but it was like she didn't hear me.

I stopped.

"Mai-*chan.*"

"My name is Mori," she said. "Mai-*chan chigau.*"

"Mori-*san.* Do you remember the time when everyone went out to do karaoke on Christmas Eve? And you sang 'Backtrack Story'? And you said you got really drunk on soda, and you fell asleep on the train?"

She shook her head.

"God gave you back to us," I said, and I don't know why I was talking like that; I told you I'm not religious. And I said *gave you back*, like you'd send back a package. "You're going to get better. And I'll be with you until you do get better—always. But I have to go away now. You might not see me again for a while. But just—try to remember that if you can. You really had fun that night."

I couldn't tell if she understood or not. It looked like she was trying to.

"Okay," she said.

And I was sorry I'd even had to make her think about what happened.

But I said I wasn't going to talk about that.

"*Sayonara*, Mai-*chan*," I said.

"*Sayonara*, Class Rep. *Sarabai.*"

I went out into the hall. Mr. Tanaka was sitting on a chair, and Mr. Neils was leaning against the wall. When I had shut the door he came up to me and said quietly, "You okay?"

I just looked at him.

"I knew it," he said and shrugged his shoulders. "I knew it."

Mr. Tanaka said, "Tohru-*kun*. How is she?"

"I think she'll get better," I said. "She remembered a lot."

I didn't know if I believed that, but I believed it enough to say it. Anyway, that was the part he was interested in.

He breathed out. "That's good."

Then I went down the hall with Mr. Neils and told him the part that *he* was interested in.

PETER NEILS

walked into the cafeteria, nice and slow. I was keeping my head together. Tohru was with me.

Detective Chao was sitting at the table, looking over his notes, with one of his guys. He hadn't brought his hard-boiled eggs with him this time, but he was smoking another cigarette, and without us being able to open the windows it had gotten pretty soupy in there.

"Ah, Mr. Neils. Officer Chien and I were just weighing the possibilities of calling an ambulance for the girl. In my estimation, it doesn't seem necessary. For one thing—"

"Listen to this," I said, and I pushed Tohru forward. "Now, tell the detective what you told me."

Tohru moved like he was sleepwalking, like he had moved ever since he had come out of that room, and he told Chao very clearly what he had told me.

Chao slowly raised one eyebrow.

"Is this the truth?"

"Why would I lie?" said Tohru.

"Why, indeed?" said Chao. He got up. "Where is he now?"

"He said he had to lie down. Beyond that I've got no clue."

"That isn't much good. Shall we go find him?"

"I'll go. Detective, have you got a gun?"

"Of course."

He was wearing a trench coat and I couldn't see it.

"Give it to me," I said.

He didn't even blink, just said, "I will not do that."

Okay, it had been a dumb thing to say, but I felt—he's *my* responsibility. I've got to deal with him.

"Then come with me."

"Mr. Neils," he said, "do not do anything rash. Remember that all we have to go on is the word of an insane girl."

I could see Tohru bristle that the detective had called the girl insane, even though it was in some way true.

"Tohru," I said, "go find your friends. Make sure they're safe."

He nodded. The detective nodded to his man, and the three of us went out, me first.

As I walked, though, I started thinking.

Not only was it the word of a—*not* insane, a very disturbed, traumatized girl—but what exactly was that word? Tohru had been clear. All she'd done was mention Pickett immediately after she mentioned the girl Kari. She didn't say Pickett the rapist, or Pickett the murderer; just Pikketto-*san*. Nice, friendly Pikketto-*san*. And Pickett was the last person she had probably seen, and he had clearly made a bigger impression on them than I had, with his flashy camera and goofy attempts to communicate.

I didn't want to make the same mistake twice. I told myself,

for the final time, that the girls had just fallen into a hole—
a kind of natural well—and that was what she had meant by
water, and somehow Mai had survived and managed to crawl to
safety.

But I kept going, down the hall, and opened the door to our
room. Pickett was lying on his bed with his back to us, facing the
wall. His shoulders looked enormous. How, I asked myself again,
had I never realized how big and strong he was?

The detective had opened his trench coat and his hands
were on the belt.

I shook my head: *Don't wake him up*. I took a step into
the room.

The lights were off, and light from outside was like a dying
bulb. The windows were translucent with rain and reflected me
and the detective as blobs.

Lying at the foot of his bed, next to two now empty bottles
of plum liquor, was Pickett's day bag. It was a little green thing
shaped like a stomach that slung over his back. Inside had been
the camera, but it was too big for just that. He had just one other
bag at the hostel, a backpack, and at least half his shit must have
been in there.

To this day I don't know what possessed me. Chao had
warned me not to do anything rash, and ordinarily I'm not the
type. I told you before: I'm an observer. But you can only watch
things for so long. Sooner or later you've got to participate.

I took Pickett's bag carefully over to my bed. The detective
and his man watched me, expressionless. I unzipped it and dumped
it out.

"Fuck," I said hoarsely.

Right there at what had been the bottom, and was now the top, there it was. Jesus, not making any *effort* to hide itself.

I held it up so they could see. Chao nodded.

"Wake him up," I said.

Chao's man went and shook Pickett by the shoulder. I watched him as he started to get up.

You sick fuck, I thought. Why did you help that girl when you knew she would tell us?

More than horrified, I felt angry. I had already processed the horror in that unbearable period of uncertainly. Now with the certainty came anger. He had looked me in the face and lied to me—and been so goddamn convincing. Crocodile tears, you sick, sick son of a bitch, you rapist, you murderer.

He looked at me. "Oh, hey, Crazy Pete. What's up?"

I held up the pair of dirty white girl's underwear.

"Pickett, you have got less than five seconds to explain this to me, and if I don't like your explanation, then believe it to hell, some shit is going down."

He stared with an open mouth. What could he say?

"Mr. Pickett, please do nothing stupid," said Chao. "Answer your friend's question."

The policeman was standing next to Pickett. He was a slim guy, and I knew if any of us had a chance of stopping Pickett, it was Chao. I may not have liked him, but I bet my life on him just then.

"Man," said the killer. "What the hell is this?"

"Answer the question," said Chao.

"Where—did—these—come—from?"

Pickett swallowed. Very slowly he said: "The girl."

"Yeah," I said. "You want to tell us about the girl? The girl you raped—and then took this *trophy*?"

I threw it at him. He caught it.

"I thought you were a good guy," I said. "You sick fuck. How could you do it? How could you even do it? Just on the spur of the moment—you decided like *that*? Those girls. Those fucking girls."

Chao nodded. His man stepped forward, displaying bravery that surprised me even in a professional, and put his hand on Pickett's arm; his tiny hand, Pickett's huge biceps.

"Come with us," he said in Mandarin.

Pickett, comprehending perfectly well the hand on his arm, looked down, eyes bleary, and muttered, "Get your fucking hand off me."

Instead the cop tightened his grip. Chao's hand went inside his jacket; I stood motionless.

"Motherfucker," said Pickett and freed his arm with a wrench.

"Mr. Pickett!"

"Fuck you, too, Charlie Chan." Then he held his head with both hands and said, "I am so sick of this shit."

He must have still been drunk—which, I had just time to reflect, made him twice as dangerous.

He took one step forward, quickly enough that I jumped back and whacked my shoulder against the doorframe, but Chao still didn't draw his gun. Instead he stepped forward.

Pickett gave a yell that was more like a sob, and pulled back his arm; I could hardly follow what happened next. Chao dropped, stomping the ground with one foot, threw his arms around Pickett's waist, and hurled all two hundred pounds of him to the floor with a crash that shook the room.

Mr. Tanaka ran in, and I put my arm in front of him. Pickett was on his back; Chao stood over him with a black pistol in both hands, his whole body tensed like a spring. Then he winced and leaned forward, and I could see one of his legs was bad, but he recovered, and Picket was just lying there moaning.

"As you people say," said Chao, "do not fuck with me."

And Pickett started laughing desperately, tears in his eyes.

"Was it him?" asked Mr. Tanaka in a whisper of incredible violence. "Was it him?"

I didn't answer. I was staring down at Pickett, and now he looked up at me.

"The girl . . ." he said.

"Tell us about the girl," I said. "Tell us what happened and maybe they won't fry you."

"Tell us," said Chao.

"The girl," he said. "From the bar."

I stopped.

"Say that again."

"The girl from the *bar*, man."

He shut his eyes and lay there with one hand on his forehead, the other still holding the balled-up underwear.

"She was into me as hell," said Pickett, as if half asleep. "And I know I'm supposed to be a Buddhist and not have desire and shit, but fuck it, it's *hard*. You get tanked and you just do anything.

"She acted all into me . . . but she was just trying to get her boyfriend jealous. The dude walked in on us; I could have snapped him in half, he was just this little Asian dude, but instead I ran like hell. Didn't even have time to take the rubber off my dick." He wheeze-laughed. "But I grabbed those. Fuck it, guess I just wanted *something*. I wasn't thinking. Man, I never think."

"Is that the truth?"

"Man. Why the fuck would I lie about something like that?"

Quietly Tanaka said, "I think it is."

"Mr. Neils," Chao said carefully, without shifting his aim, "is there any truth in this story?"

"It could be true," I said.

Then I looked in Pickett's eyes and knew that it was. There was no falsehood there, just a scared, hurt young man, and then not even that.

"Is that all you've got?" he said.

Me on the defensive now. All I could do was stare at him.

"If you'd *asked* me," he said, "I could have told you nobody messed with that girl. You think I didn't *check*?" He laughed again. "And if you'd looked at her, you'd have seen those cuts, man, they were consistent with her falling down some rocks and in no fucking way with anyone attacking her. And if you'd been there—man—you'd have seen when she woke up, the way she looked at me. Like I was an angel, man. And she said, 'Pikketto-*san*.'

"'Pikketto-*san*.'

"I fell in love with those girls, Pete. I would've given my own life for them. And you think I raped them."

"Pickett . . ."

"Fucking throw me down, fucking point a gun at me . . ."

"You looked like you were going to hit him," I said, but I knew it had just been the booze and stress.

"No, man. Don't say anything."

But then, again, he was spent. He couldn't stay angry for long. He was young, and it wasn't in his nature.

What else could I say? That I was sorry? But how could I make up for *this*? I think there was no way. I had doubted him right down to the core of his self, and it was like he hadn't existed for me. Now there was no way we could even communicate.

I looked in his eyes and he was dead inside, and I had killed him.

Chao let his gun drop, put it back in the holster, and stepped away.

"Mr. Pickett," he said, "it seems there has been a mistake. Allow me to apologize on our behalf. . . ."

"What the shit *was* that?"

"Of course you understand that we had to be careful."

Shut up, I thought; you're making it worse.

"Josh," I said, "I understand you're mad at me. Look, I believe you." And I turned to go.

Suddenly his eyes widened. "Wait."

I stopped.

"I said I trust you, Josh. We're good."

"No, man." He shook his head. "You don't trust me. You just don't think I did it."

"Mr. Pickett, you have to understand that the circumstantial evidence against you did seem quite strong. You were named by the young lady who—"

"She named me?"

"Well . . ." I said. "That's not quite what she said."

"Well, fuck, man."

He got slowly to his feet, brushed his arms, swayed, then clutched his head again. In spite of everything, I flinched. Chao took another step back, and Tanaka, who was standing in the door, moved quickly to one side.

"Pickett, don't do anything stupid."

"Fuck it. I been doing nothing but stupid shit my whole life."

And he walked past us. Just before he left the room, he put his hand awkwardly on Tanaka's shoulder—Tanaka jumped—and said, to him but not to the rest of us, "I understand how you feel, man."

The door shut behind him.

Chao called, "Ms. Zhu? Ms. Zhu!"

In a minute the young parks lady, who had—I think wisely—been battened down somewhere during these proceedings, came in timidly.

"Detective?"

He leaned toward her and whispered in her ear. She turned red.

"Will you go and do this? It is very important," he said in Mandarin.

She nodded.

"What is it; what did you tell her?"

But he didn't tell me and she was gone, her heels clicking, and there was no sign of Pickett, and we stood there like the bunch of idiots we were.

Chao was mopping sweat off his wrinkled old face. "Don't blame yourself," he said to me, as goddamn superior as ever. "I would have come to the same conclusion. And what is more, I myself looked at the girl's clothing, and it seemed possible to me that it was torn by human hands. But it is just as possible that it was torn when she had a fall."

"You don't understand. That guy was my friend."

"Sometimes we don't know what men are capable of. Initially I had a quite strong suspicion of *you*, for several reasons. But now I no longer have this suspicion."

"What changed your mind?"

"Nothing specifically. I can only say that it no longer seems likely."

"Then what do you think happened?"

He shook his head.

After a pause Tanaka, standing there flexing his knuckles, asked, "That thing you did. Where did you learn it?"

"Oh? Every man in Taiwan has to do sixteen months in the army. I did five years on top of that."

"It wasn't bad."

"Thank you."

Ms. Zhu came back. She looked very embarrassed, but when Chao looked at her she nodded, and she said something to him—quietly—in Mandarin.

Chao looked at me. "The girl has not been interfered with."

Was I glad to hear that? Of course I was.

But let's be honest. Hadn't a part of me—even back then, when I told myself it was too horrible to consider—hadn't a part of me *wanted* it to be true? Because if it were true, there would be an answer.

I nodded.

Chao looked at his watch. "I suggest we take a short rest to gather ourselves and then—begin our search. I assume that you want to come with us, Mr. Neils."

"That's right."

"Then I will see you in ten minutes."

The two cops and Ms. Zhu went out and left me alone.

I sat down on my bed. The contents of Pickett's bag were still spilled all over it. A tortoiseshell comb—what the hell use did he have for a comb, maybe it was to remind him of some girlfriend—a couple dollars in change, both Taiwanese and American; a pocket flash drive; one extra shirt and one pair of socks; a Swiss Army pocketknife; two condoms, still joined together; and, for all they had pissed him off, a couple of charms from the temple. So he was a disorganized bastard just like me.

It was like Chao had said, you don't know what even your friends are capable of; it isn't really possible to trust anyone *completely*. Hell, you can't even trust yourself.

I hadn't come out and told Pickett I was sorry because I didn't think he was ready to hear it. Since then not a day of my life has gone by that I don't regret that.

I found him in the kitchen. He had located another bottle of that plum liquor and was already more than halfway in the bag. Yesterday's olive shirt, his camouflage pants, and the sweat running off his arms.

I don't know why I went after him; there was no question of him joining our search party. Maybe I was afraid that like Chao had said, he'd do something stupid.

"Pickett, give me the bottle."

He looked at me with his frog-like pithed eyes.

"No way, man."

"Give it here."

I reached for it, but he pulled it back.

"Come on," I said, trying to sound friendly. "Don't do this to yourself. You've been sober for about four hours these past two days. Why don't you go lie back down, huh?"

"The hell do you care?"

"Josh"—again—"I want it to be cool with us. We both know the truth now."

He was leaning with one arm on the stove, the bottle in his other hand. The top of his head almost brushed the ceiling.

"Forget you, man," petulant like a child.

"Josh," I said, "I know you're not completely tanked yet, so I know you'll understand me. I want to tell you something. It's something I didn't tell you before—something I haven't told anyone in, like, years. Okay?"

He stared at me. "Okay."

"It's about my son," I said. "Steve."

"Steve . . . ?"

He didn't remember, so I took out my wallet again and showed him the pictures. Steve in his blue trunks sitting in the pool. Steve in khaki shorts, standing on the patio.

"You know I was married?"

"Well, duh; you've got a kid."

"That's right. And I told you I hadn't seen him in years, didn't I? Well, this is why."

"I'm listening," said Pickett.

"The thing is . . . my wife and I, we didn't get along too well. You know how it is—or well, maybe you don't, but you could guess. We got married too young. By the time I had a job and the kid was born, well, we were different people. We couldn't re-member why we'd gotten married. And I guess that happens to a lot of people, and they get through it, but . . . the thing is, I drank. Obviously. Shit, it's not like I've changed that much. It's an old story; I guess it happens to a lot of people."

"Uh-huh," said Pickett.

The bottle hung there in his hand. I couldn't tell if he was getting me or not, but I went on.

"When Steve was about sixteen, he started drinking, too. We were in New York by then, Queens, and he'd go out and meet all kinds of people. Come home late smelling like cheap-ass—shit. I don't even know what they call it. The kind of wine that's so cheap you could wash your car with it—Thunderbird, that shit. And I knew it was my fault, and Diane knew it was my fault, so I couldn't say anything. It went on for about a year.

"Then one night he came back at about four in the morning just trashed to hell, and I woke up. I'd had a little to drink myself that night, and I met him in the front hall. Well you can probably guess what happened. We started screaming at each other, blah, blah—you got no respect, well you're never home anyway you call yourself my dad, well if you weren't such an ungrateful shit maybe I'd be home more—just the usual bullshit, and of course he let me know whose fault it was, and because I *knew* damn well it was all my fault, I just let him have it—right in the face. Seventeen years old and he went down like a rock.

"I started beating the shit out of him. My own kid. There

was a baseball bat there, *his* bat, and I started hitting him with it. So Diane came in in her nightgown and grabbed me and started crying, and it is just a god*damn* good thing—I don't even know how it happened, maybe it was a miracle—I didn't take her head off with that bat. I just pushed her down and ran out. Ran away like *I* was the kid. I spent the night in some motel, I don't even remember which.

"Well . . . she didn't call the cops. That's not how we did things back home; you took care of your own problems. When I came back the next day, she let me in—oh, I was surprised, believe me—sat me right down and said Steve was in the hospital, and she was getting a divorce. I said that was fine by me. I never wanted to see that stupid kid again, or her. I was just glad as hell she didn't have me arrested. As far as the cops knew, well, the culprit was New York's most prolific criminals—two unidentified black guys."

I wiped my forehead.

"Since then, I've . . . well I guess you could say I feel different. I send her the check every month. I never missed *one* goddamn month, not even when I was in Ne*pal*. And I write to her, and usually she doesn't write back, but I keep writing, and sometimes she will—just to let me know they're okay. She told me they let Steve out of the hospital; all he had was a fractured arm. Like I said, I guess it's kind of a miracle; I could have killed him, easy.

"So . . . just give me the goddamn bottle, Josh. You do shit you regret."

Pickett looked at me and said, "You are one fucked-up guy."

"It was thirteen years ago," I said. "I've changed."

Then we were both quiet.

"After it happened," I said, "I mean, *long* enough after that I could get some fucking perspective . . . I swore to God it would never happen again. But I feel like—now, I wasn't drunk or anything this time, but I feel like it happened again. I let my temper get the better of me and—I messed you up. It's nothing personal, Josh. That's . . . just the way I am."

"What, you think I'm your son?" said Pickett.

I shrugged. "You're young enough to be."

"Okay," he said. "That's cool."

He took a big, big swig.

"Pickett—"

"Fuck," he said, and he was slurring now, "'s'not your fault. 'S'mine. Dropped so much acid I bet my brain is like fucking Swiss cheese, man. Who drops a camera into a . . . ? Nah, man, that was me, not you. Fuck it. Maybe I *did* rape those girls. I might've blacked out."

"Don't do *this* shit. I'm trying to say—"

Then he laughed. I thought maybe it was a good sign.

"Ya know what, Crazy Pete?"

"What, man?"

"You stay on the bus," he said. "Stay on the motherfucking bus."

I went for the bottle again, but this time he danced away, agile as hell for a drunk guy, and sang, "The End": "*The blue bu-us . . . is calling u-us. . . .*"

"Josh don't be an asshole. Give it here."

He ducked and swerved around me.

"*The blue bu-us . . .* I played ball in college. Think you can keep up, old man? Didn't believe I'd been an EMT. Fuck, man, I'm from Cali; I done a bit of everything."

Then he ran out of the room, and I ran after him.

"Detective!" I screamed. "Detective!"

Pickett was just too fast for me. Right out of the kitchen, down the hall, and into the big foyer, where I chased him around the pillars feeling simultaneously like an idiot and scared to death; then he stopped and tipped back the bottle—

"Ah-come on baby take a chance with us. . . ."

He was on one side of the pillar and I was on the other. Then he faked me out and ran straight at the door, wailing like god-damn Morrison himself, *"Come on baby take a chance with us, and—meet me at the back of the—blu-ue bus, doin' a blue rock on a blue bus, doin' a—blue rock, come on* ye-ah!"

"Pickett Jesus Christ!"

I stood there knowing that if I moved he'd be out the door. *"Detective!"*

"Come on baby, come on baby . . . fuck me baby, fuck, fuck . . . !"

He looked right in my eyes.

"Pickett," I said.

"Fuck, ye-eah!"

I lunged. He went right through the door; then Chao ran in and I looked around, and by the time I looked back the door was swinging shut and he was gone—out into that storm, that physical definition of insanity.

"Let it go," said Chao.

"Are you out of your mind? You saw how it is out there."

"Yes. And that is why I say let it go."

"But—!"

"We will look for him when we look for the others—all of us, together."

I threw the door open and screamed, *"Pickett! Pickett! Pickett!"*

I couldn't see the trees for the rain. It slapped me in the face and the wind tried to tear my jacket off. The power of that storm was like nothing ever, and I knew right then that it had eaten him alive, but still I stood there screaming, *Pickett, Pickett.*

MICHIKO KAMAKIRI

kay, I admit it. I lied.

Twice. I lied twice. But one time was just leaving something out.

There are different kinds of lies you can tell. The kind where you just leave something out and the kind where you make something up. To make someone think something happened, or to *keep* them from thinking something happened. Then there are the kinds of lies you tell to other people and the ones you tell to yourself—just like to make things neater. The kind that don't really *change* anything, they just make things neater. Little lies. But you tell enough of them, and things can change a lot. And sometimes a lie you tell to someone else is a lie you also tell to yourself. You keep telling it long enough, and pretty soon you start believing it—and just forget about what really happened.

So I lied, and then I lied about lying because I didn't say anything about it. And I don't know, for a long time I almost forgot about it. But then I saw Mai.

I didn't go straight back to the bus after I came up from the river. That was what I told everyone, but nobody saw us leave. The truth is, I started walking with Kari, Taeko, and Mai. It doesn't really make sense that I would go right back, does it?—not even wondering where they were going. That's kind of stupid, isn't it?

The truth is, Kari asked me what I'd been up to. Then I had an idea. I'd been up *there*, I said. In the jungle.

"Wow," Taeko-*chan* said, "isn't that dangerous?"

"Nah, I wasn't scared. And I saw something really cool."

"What, what?" said Taeko-*chan*.

Then I kind of had to think on my feet. I said, "A deer. It was really big and pretty."

And Taeko-*chan* started jumping and clapping her hands: "Let's go, let's go!"

"I don't know," said Kari, but then Mai said *she'd* like to see it, and I said it totally wasn't dangerous at all. There was a path and everything—and I knew that from looking at the brochure.

And I took out the brochure and pointed at where I'd seen this deer.

That was all.

It's not like it was my fault. I didn't tell them to go jumping off a cliff, or into a hole in the fabric of space. People walk on those paths all the time, so how was I supposed to know it was dangerous? I just wanted to get Kari out of there because it bugged me the way Class Rep kept hanging on her, and how she had been so *nice* to me. And maybe while she was gone, I could get in a word with Class Rep because I'd been checkmated by stupid Chizu with Sumiregawa.

What's so wrong about that?

Like I said, nice girls finish last. In the psy-ops book for junior high girls, subterfuge is an acceptable tactic. It wasn't even *that* mean because they'd never know I'd lied; they'd just think they hadn't seen the stupid deer. I hadn't like promised it would still be there or anything.

When they all asked me about it, right there outside the temple, all of them looking at me—I couldn't really say that part. But leaving it out didn't *change* anything; the important thing was that they had walked off, and I knew what direction, and I showed them. I really wanted them to find those losers, and I got scared when they didn't; of course I was just as scared as anyone. I never, *ever* wanted this to happen, and it's what you mean that counts, right? You can't be responsible for everything that happens because of what you do.

So that was the second lie. And I got really scared when everyone was yelling at me, because I *hadn't* done it, but it would be bad if they found out about that lie; but then Class Rep stepped in and it was okay. For a while it was okay because he believed me, and so for I while I guess *I* kind of believed me, too.

Then I stopped thinking about it, and it was like it hadn't happened. When nobody knows anything, it's like your lie can really change what happened. But then as soon as I saw Mai, I knew, I remembered, what goes around comes around, and it was all over.

I knew I had to make it up, and I would. No one would know about it because I would do it in secret; I would pay Mai-*chan's* bills at the hospital and carry her books and stuff when she got back to school, like I was just being a friend. I'd be nice to her for the rest of her life.

I'm not a bad girl! Please, you've got to believe me. I just want normal things, the same things as everyone else. It isn't my fault I was born without big breasts, or really smart, or really brave. I just wanted to have nice things. Nice things—like I had now.

Then I knew I had to tell someone. Just one person. The one person who really cared about me.

When we got back, it was obvious Koizumi had almost lost his mind. Everyone had. I was, well, I mean I had other things to think about, and it hadn't even occurred to me they'd be worried about us. When it started raining I couldn't believe it, but it was just one more thing that *happened*, one more crazy thing.

Koizumi kept hugging me and rubbing my shoulders. It made me scared. How could I tell him?—and it was so weird that just because I knew he cared about me, and I could tell him, it was so hard to tell him.

But finally I did.

We went off, and nice Ms. Zhu ran all around to get cups of hot tea for us and even brought some clothes she said had been in the lost and found. It was all mixed up. Sumiregawa got some bright blue shorts and a sweatshirt, and I got a dress shirt and some men's pants that were way too long. Even thinking about what I was thinking about, I wondered how anyone could lose their pants there. I guess they dropped their bag.

Then Ms. Zhu left us alone, and we were in the guys' room. I was sitting on Koizumi's lap with my arms around him. Sumiregawa sat cross-legged and put his cigarette pack on his knee and took one out and held a match underneath it to dry it out. He did it all so calmly he looked like a soldier.

"You *smoke*?" said Koizumi.

"Our little secret," he said.

"Man, whatever. When we get back, you guys are gonna be total heroes. If *you're* too modest to tell, I will! We should have a school ceremony or something."

Sumiregawa flapped his hand. "I'd just as soon you kept quiet about it."

"No, really!" Then he said, "It's weird to think about going back."

"Yeah," I whispered, and Sumiregawa nodded.

"It seems like this rain is never going to stop," he said.

"I couldn't believe it! Why'd it have to rain *today* . . . ? But that's why you guys are such heroes. They're not gonna believe it when I tell them."

"I wonder how much of this we *can* tell them," said Sumiregawa.

"What do you mean?"

"For most people . . ." He paused, and the smoke drifted out of his mouth. "It's better to simplify things. Skillful means."

Koizumi scratched his head. "Maybe you're right. Like you and Mr. Tanaka smoking; I'd leave *that* part out."

Sumiregawa smiled.

Then I pulled on Koizumi's sleeve and said as quietly as I could, "Hey. Can I talk to you, like—alone for a little while?"

"Uh, sure."

He got all red. Oh, God, if not for everything it would have been so cute.

Sumiregawa just sat there smoking.

"Umm, we'll be back in a minute," said Koizumi.

"Don't overdo it," he said, kind of mysteriously. Koizumi just gave a weird chuckle.

I said, "Seiji-*kun*, hey . . . you were really brave back there."

"You were pretty brave yourself," he said.

It felt good to hear that.

Then he went all quiet. I wondered if what had happened had maybe changed the way he thought about things. For a second there, it sure had looked like he believed in ghosts.

We went to my room, holding hands. We still didn't know what to do around each other. It was so stupid—if we'd just known each other a few more days before *this*. Inside he stopped me and said, "Eh, Michiko-*san*. Y-you don't have anything in *mind*—huh?"

It was kind of stupid, like he was joking with a guy.

"No," I said, all serious. "I just want it like last night."

"Okay," he said.

And he put his arms around me. It felt so good, I can't even say.

So this was what I was missing all those years. I didn't care about "other stuff"; this was good for now, it was everything I had hoped for. Just lying there on the sleeping bag with my nose touching his nose. Even in those stupid clothes I was wearing.

"Koizumi," I said.

He was hoarse. "Yeah?"

"Do you like me?"

"Of course I like you." He gave me a squeeze. "I love you."

"That's good," I said. "It makes me really happy to hear that. Really, really happy."

"Well, it makes me happy to say it. I'm really, really happy, too."

"The thing is . . . there's one thing I've got to tell you."

I felt him tighten up. But what could he think it was? That I was seeing someone else? That I was really a guy? He just had no idea. But he said, "Sure, anything."

"Just promise me. Promise me when I tell you, no matter what it is, you won't let go of me. Okay? Because that would make me feel . . . really bad."

"Yakusoku da." It's a promise.

So I told him.

Right away he let go of me and sat up straight.

"Koizumi! You promised me."

"Michiko-*san*," he said, and his voice was shaking.

Then I played it all wrong. I kind of tried to joke about it, grabbing him and saying, "I knew I could tell you; I just knew my wonderful boyfriend would understand . . . that it wasn't *my* fault, right?"

I was rubbing my face on his shoulder.

"Michiko-*san*, this isn't joking around. This is serious."

I pulled back. "You think I don't know that?"

He looked at me. And in that second everything good turned bad. Like that scene in *Mononoke Hime*, where the good spirit turns bad and he touches the trees and they all start to die.

"Koizumi."

"Don't touch me," he said.

"Koizumi-*kun*!"

"When they brought in Mai-*chan*," he said, "I saw her face."

"I saw it, too; I was *there*—"

"*You* did that. It was you."

"No! No! Weren't you *listening*? I didn't, I didn't *mean* to, how could I—"

And there he was. Peacemaker Koizumi. Koizumi the fair guy, the mature guy.

"Michiko-*san*," he said, "that's what you felt."

"But I *didn't* feel that way! Don't you understand? I didn't like her, but I didn't *hate* her; I never wanted her to—" *die*— "disappear like that."

He shook his head. "It doesn't matter. What you did was enough." Then, with just a little feeling, he said, "I can't believe it."

He'd started calling me *anta* instead of *kimi*. How can I even explain that? It's like if he stopped calling me *darling* and started calling me *hey, you*.

"Koizumi." I tried to grab him, and he pulled back. "I know it was wrong! I'm not saying I didn't do anything wrong. I told you I'm sorry. I'll do whatever it takes to make it up. . . ."

"How—?" He choked. "How could you ever make up for *that*?"

Mai-*chan*'s face. Her lying on that rock, looking up at the sky. With the puffy white face of a dead girl.

"I'm sorry," I said. "I'm sorry, I'm sorry."

"Don't tell it to me. It doesn't do me any good."

He started to get up.

"Where are you going!"

"To tell Class Rep."

"You *can't*!"

"It's the right thing to do."

I grabbed his leg, and even when he tried to get away, I held on.

"Don't. Don't go."

"Look at yourself," he said. "You're so scared of being caught. You thought I'd be your—*accomplice*?"

I remembered awful Ogami-*san*. *Witnesses*. Witnesses, Koizumi had said; Ogami, *listen* to yourself.

"No! It's not that. Koizumi. Look at me. Listen to me."

He didn't move.

"You said I was pretty," I said with my face buried in the leg of his pants. "You said you liked me. You said you'd liked me forever. Then you said you loved me. Everything you said—were you lying?"

"Michiko-*san*," he said, "*antatte bishijin. Sugoku kirei da. Shikashi, anta no kokorotte kirei janai.*"

The thing is, it sounds kind of stupid in English. What he'd said was, Michiko, you're a beautiful girl. You are really pretty. But your heart isn't pretty.

I started crying.

"You girls," he said. "You always cry to get what you want."

And now I was close to being as mad at him as he was at me. But I was still in love with him. Then I thought of something that gave me just the tiniest bit of hope. I thought maybe it was the same with him—that he was mad at me and he liked me still. But if that was true, he wasn't showing it.

"Koizumi," I said, "Koizumi, please, please, *onegai, onegai, onegaishimasu*."

He shrugged. "What do you want me to do?"—Then his face got calm and he said, "Okay. I won't tell Class Rep."

I screamed. I held on to his leg like I would break it, and finally he sat back down, and I threw myself on his lap and cried and cried.

"What's the matter?" he said. "That's what you wanted, isn't it?"

"Koizumi . . . *onegai*. Just listen to me. Just listen to me say one thing."

He was quiet a long, long time, but then he said, "Okay."

My head was on his leg, turned sideways. He couldn't see my face.

"I've always been alone," I said. "I don't care how cheesy that sounds—it's true. I don't have any brothers or sisters. All day, all night, Mom and Dad just worked. And I got along with everyone, but I never had a lot of friends. All I had was the stupid clarinet."

"If you're just trying to get me to feel sorry for you . . ."

"*No*! No. I'm just trying . . . to explain."

"Okay," he said. "Okay."

"Koizumi," I said, "you've got to believe me. I'm sorry as *any-thing* it happened. But I was just . . . so . . . jealous. Stupid Kari had everything. I just got tired of being a loser. I wanted to be a winner . . . for just one time in my life. And I did win! Because I found you. A person who makes me happy. A person who likes me. I wasn't alone anymore. And I knew I never would be because I would always, always be with you. You've got to believe me. It made me so happy I could die."

"It isn't fair," he said quietly, and oh—his voice was *different*. "That's Kari's happiness, Michiko. You took it from her."

"I know," I said. "But I can't help that! I told you I couldn't help anything. I know it isn't fair. It was *too late*—that's it. I won, but it was too late."

"Michiko-*san*."

"I don't care about you telling Class Rep. I just got scared because—to think that *you*, my special person, would do something like that—to me."

"Michiko-*san*," he said.

He wanted me to look at him, but I couldn't, not until I was sure. He had to understand, no matter what.

I had started rubbing my cheek up and down his leg as I talked. I put my hand on his knee and let it move up, still not looking at him, feeling him get all stiff. Then I *really* felt something.

He was breathing hard and so was I. I moved my fingers in tiny circles.

"You believe me," I said. "Don't you?"

I looked up.

"Don't you?"

He shut his eyes. "I believe you."

Thank you. Just thank you, Whoever.

Then he was crying and he leaned down and kissed me, and it lasted for a long time. Then he pulled back.

"M-Michiko-*san*," he said. "How *could* you do it?"

That was when I realized it would never go away. It would never, ever *really* go away. For my whole life it would be there, whether I spent it with Koizumi or not. And maybe that was what I deserved.

"I'm sorry," I said. "I'm sorry."

But how can I explain? It's like you were a son or a daughter of a big house. And one day your parents kicked you out of the house, and you were there on the street. Day in, day out, you sat in front of the gate hoping they'd let you in. And then finally one day they did. You're going to be our slave from now on, they said, and do the cooking and cleaning and all the nastiest jobs. But you were just so, so glad to be let into the house again.

That was what it was like.

I understood. I would do everything I could to make up for it in little ways, knowing I could never make up for it. It would be with me forever, and now I would never be alone because Kari, Taeko, and Mai would be with me. But that was how it had to be.

After a long time Koizumi said, "We can't tell anyone."

I shook my head. "No. No. They wouldn't understand like you do."

But then again.

Why does it have to be that way? Don't I have a right to be happy?

Of course I'll do what I can. Of course I feel really bad; you can't imagine. Of course I know I can never really make up for it. Not a day will go by when I don't see Mai's face. But *can't I be happy* anyway; can't I try? Why should I have to be unhappy forever just because of something that happened by accident? It doesn't do *them* any good. I bet they would *want* me to be happy. I know Kari would want me to be happy.

That's it. Kari always wanted what was best for everyone. She would even . . . I bet she would even kill herself if it meant doing something good. This happened, and it was awful, sad, terrible, but I think she would be glad that I found Koizumi because of it, and that I can be happy now.

I'm not going to be a loser anymore. I'm going to make a future for myself with Koizumi—always and forever. I'll do everything I can for Mai-*chan*. I'll be friends with Class Rep and Sumiregawa-*san*. And I'll go to high school, and college, and get a good job, or maybe just stay home and take care of the kids, I haven't decided.

We'll have a real house with a yard. A car. A dog—I love dogs. Koizumi will come home from work and I'll have dinner ready, even if I do work, and he'll never drink or cheat on me, and we'll always be just as much in love as we are now.

Why shouldn't I? Who's going to tell me I shouldn't?

I'm sorry, I'm sorry, I'm sorry, but I've got to leave this behind. I've got to live my life, I've got to keep going. And that means I've got to leave *you* behind. I'm sorry.

Good-bye, Kari Hiraoka. I mean it! Good-bye!

Sarabai!

PETER NEILS

Most missing-persons cases are solved within the first forty-eight hours or not at all. Sometimes you hear thirty-six hours. That gets thrown around a lot, but it's the truth.

Detective Chao had come out partly to grandstand, I'm sure. But he also came because every passing hour decreased the chances of ever finding the girls alive by some huge fraction. Each hour of searching was worth buying with blood. So we searched.

The rain and the wind weren't *things* anymore; they were the air. It was a world that attacked you every moment with its every particle. The way you have to get used to breathing and moving your legs, we had to get used to being rocked by the wind and hammered by the rain, all the while under the threat of a tree or rock toppling on us. But you couldn't keep an eye out for that; you couldn't think about that. You had to keep your eye on the yellow poncho in front of you. If the guy behind you lost sight of you, that was it for him. The only thing you could do was yell.

"Kari!"

"Taeko!"

"Pickett!"

Pickett.

Taeko.

Kari.

The names lost their meaning. They were just sounds you made, and not even that, because the wind snatched them out of your mouth the second you made them. I could barely hear myself, let alone anyone else.

We went up the path through the trees. A guy slipped, and the guy behind him helped him up as quickly as he could, because if you stopped a tree was sure to fall. We followed the path until it split and then split again, pulling galoshes out of ankle-deep mud and stabbing our feet on the rocks embedded in it, daring a look to the left or right, and then we were on the road and we followed it. A wave of water several inches high washed over the road and down, into the gorge. We sneaked a look. The wall of the gorge was dead gray past the rain. In most places it was smooth, but here and there were caves, huge, gaping holes in the rock like burrows of things from horror movies, ancient caves no one had explored and come back alive. Search? Who was searching? We were looking at what amounted to one square inch of the place. It went on for miles aboveground, and miles more underground, and there we were crawling down the road in fear for our own lives.

We were looking for anyone. We could have been survivors of an ecological disaster, looking for one other human soul. I don't know what might have happened had someone answered us. We probably would have lost our minds, thinking that, like the kids who'd found the one girl, we were seeing a ghost. The whole thing was as insane and futile as the deaths that Hemingway described in the Andalusians. You live like a dog and you die like something worse than a dog.

We searched because then we could say that we had searched. I'm sure we were already rehearsing the words. *We went out in the storm; we looked for hours.* There was nothing more we could do.

Kari.

Taeko.

Pickett.

A few times I think I even called *Mai* because a part of her, even the better part, surely was still lost out there.

Through the whole day, and the night before, I had never once thought about going home. But during those three hours, I did. I tried to keep the thoughts out, but they kept coming: taking a hot bath, Bushmills from a cut-glass tumbler, a good cigar. Feeding the pigeons that landed on the air conditioner. Taking my time. Before then it hadn't occurred to me that I was under no obligation to suffer like this. But suddenly I knew and appreciated that I had a home, a place to go back to. So did the detective. So did Mr. Tanaka and the kids. Cheers, where everybody knows your name. I had always gone out and put myself through these tortures, looking for something that was always somewhere else. And telling the story. That was the job. But now I started to think about home.

I felt a powerful stab of guilt. I knew it meant I had given up hope.

But we did find something. Far off on the road, it was a green shape through the rain, a paler green than the ruined foliage.

The detective said something I couldn't hear, and we broke rank and ran forward, kicking against the water. When we were ten feet off, it became obvious what it was. The detective stopped. I stopped. He put his hand on my arm.

What did he think I was going to do, throw myself into the river? Maybe, for once, it was a simple human gesture on his part.

Pickett was lying on the road facedown in half a foot of water. It kept washing over his back and head. The liquor bottle was smashed in his hand. He was too heavy for the water to float over the edge, down into the river.

I knew he was dead even though I thought he couldn't possibly be. You don't drown in six inches of moving water. Pickett had just fallen over and hit his head. But he kept lying there, making no resistance at all to the blows of the water, to the attack of that world we had been resisting furiously for an hour.

How the hell does something like that even happen? He was young and strong. We were a bunch of old guys and we were still alive. But he was sick and drunk, and I could imagine it too well: the shoulders dropping from exhaustion, the wet clothes hanging like iron, until some part of him finally decided there was no more putting up with this shit. You keep getting up until you can't anymore. And then your body just decides, *Fuck it.*

Pikketto-*san!*

Fuck it.

The detective and I tried to haul him up. He must have weighed two hundred pounds. We lifted him and I saw the gray face, and phlegmy water poured from his mouth and nose. Then another guy grabbed him under the hips and we started to carry him. The unspoken assumption was that we couldn't leave him there, even though he wasn't going anywhere. I carried him with my hands under both his shoulders, looking down at his face as his head bounced up and down, watching the water drizzling out of his mouth.

What did you come here for? I thought. The job? Just to have some fun? Did you ever, in your wildest dreams, imagine that you would end up in a goddamn puddle on the road? What fucked-up chain of circumstances brought you here, Pickett, what possible reason?

Because of the rain it took a long time for me to realize I was crying. When I did, I signaled to Chao with my head that I was tired, and somebody else took over.

What had brought *me* there? What had brought Mr. Tanaka or Detective Chao? Forget about three girls who'd disappeared— the question was, what the hell were any of us doing there in the first place?

Jesus, Pickett. Jesus Christ.

When we got back to the lodge, the scene from earlier was reversed. This time it was the kids who held the door open for us and watched in horror as we staggered in.

"Pikketto-*san*," said the girl Michiko.

"Don't look!" I said. "Just do yourselves a *goddamn* favor and don't look!"

But what a stupid thing to say. Of course they would look, and all the more once I said that. Tohru. Koizumi. The girl. The boy with the ponytail. Mr. Tanaka. Ms. Zhu was the only one who screamed.

And where the hell were we going to put him? A sopping-wet dead man.

"Who's looking after the sick girl?" I said. "Somebody? Hey?"

Tohru nodded to me and took off running. Koizumi took the girl's arm and they went off, too. The boy with the ponytail stayed.

We put Pickett down right there in the foyer, and two of the policemen came back with a blue tarp that we spread over him. The impression of his body showed but not his face.

"We can't just leave him there."

"Do you have a better idea, Mr. Neils?"

I looked the detective right in the eye.

"You cold bastard."

He looked away. "I sympathize with your loss," he said.

What the hell do you know about loss? I was about to say— but that was ridiculous. He must have been sixty years old. Of course he knew what loss was. I brushed my hands together. They were still spongy from the rain.

"Perhaps you should take a rest, Mr. Neils."

"Fuck you."

"I strongly advise it."

"Okay, I will."

In the room, I lay down on my bed. I listened to the rain pound the wall. It felt good to be back inside.

Pickett's shit was still there. His condoms were right by my elbow. The comb, empty of whatever obscure meaning it had had for him. And one other thing—a cell phone.

In the dark I turned it on, and the gentle glow from the screen was comforting, in a weird way. It was a new fancy cell phone with a camera, a fliptop, and a big screen. The desktop image was a picture of Pickett with his arm around the neck of a big German shepherd. And what do you know, there was a signal: three bars. Just enough to get through to someone.

I thought about going through his contacts. *Hi, I'm not Josh, my name is Peter Neils. I'm sorry to tell you Josh is dead—he died a stupid death in a rainstorm on the other side of the world, and I tried all I could, but there was nothing I could do. I'm sorry.* Who would that be? His mother? His sister? His girlfriend? I didn't even know if he had any of those.

Instead I dialed another number.

Four rings and he picked up.

"Hello?"

"Hi, Tom," I said. Using a dead man's minutes.

"Peter!" he said.

"What's the haps, you choirboy?"

"Peter, you sound awful. What's going on?"

So I told him; I told him the story. Everything that had happened since the last time. When I finished he was quiet for a while.

"Hey, Tom. What time is it there?"

"Five-thirty in the morning."

"Shit. Did I wake you up?"

"I wake up at five," he said. "I have a train to the country in an hour. Well . . . actually it doesn't leave till eight, but you've got to get there pretty early to deal with the crowds."

"Uh-huh."

"You know, the red tape and all."

"Preach it, brother. Is Min Ling there?"

"No, she's at the site."

"That's a shame. It's been forever since I talked to her."

"I haven't seen her myself in over a week."

"Is the sun up there?"

"Not quite. It's starting to get a little bright outside."

"It's raining where I am."

"Yes . . . you said."

We were quiet again.

"Peter," he said, "do you want to talk about it?"

"I did talk about it."

"I'm not altogether sure what *I* can say. But . . . if you want to talk more."

"I guess I do." I sighed and shifted around on the bed. I looked at the windows. "Why the hell else would I have called? But I don't know what to say, either."

"Peter, you know if there were anything I could do . . ."

"Yeah. I know."

He was silent.

"Tom," I said, "how the hell do you stand it?"

Somehow he knew what I meant.

"I find consolation."

"Where?"

"In my work. With Min Ling. With friends—like you."

"With God?"

"Well," he said, after a pause, "it's complicated."

"How so?"

"Peter . . . if you're asking me to give you a theological explanation for everything, well, I'm not sure I could do it, and I'm not sure it's what you'd want anyway."

"Hit me."

"If I start quoting scripture," he said, "will you hang up on me?"

I laughed. "Not this time."

"Alright, then. This is something I was reading only last night. In fact, it came to mind as soon as you called. . . ." I heard pages rustling. I could imagine the Bible right there at his elbow, always. "This is from the trial story in the Gospel of John. You might know that John's Jesus is, well, more powerful and divine, less human than in the other gospels. . . ."

"Just give me a simplified version, okay?"

"Alright, then."

"And this ain't that King James shit, is it? I can't follow that."

"No, it's NRSV. So Jesus is brought before Pilate, and Pilate asks him what he's done. Jesus says, 'My kingdom is not of this world. If my kingdom were of this world, my followers would be fighting to keep me from being handed over to the Jews. But as it is, my kingdom is not from here.'

"And Pilate asks him, 'Are you a king?' And Jesus says, 'You say that I am a king. For this I was born, and for this I came into this world, to testify to the truth. Everyone who belongs to the truth listens to my voice.'

"And Pilate asks him, 'What is truth?'"

Silence.

"So?" I finally said. "What did the man say?"

"That's the end of the chapter. We don't know what he said—if anything."

"You're shitting me."

"No. That's the way it is."

"So are you telling me . . . that even *Jesus* didn't know?"

"I'm saying that Pontius Pilate was a highly educated man, a governor. But Jesus didn't think he could explain it to him in terms that he would understand."

"Well, shit."

"Peter, you mentioned before William of Ockham. . . ."

"I didn't even know there *was* a William of Ockham. I thought Occam's Razor was like Murphy's Law."

"I'll try to boil this down . . . but in the Middle Ages, the great figure was Thomas Aquinas, and he said that God was principally reason—reason*able*—and that divine things were able to be comprehended by human reason. Then Duns Scotus came along and said that reason *wasn't* fully able to comprehend divine things because God's logic was different from man's. Then Ockham came along and blew the whole thing up. He said that reason maybe had nothing to do with God and that God wasn't reason—God wasn't a *mind*—God was Will. Completely irrational

Will. And there was no understanding Him, and who knows why He does the things He does."

"It's possible that no one did more to destroy the authority of the church than Ockham. Some people think he was a heretic. And the Thomist position is more popular these days—*in the church*. But in the world it's Ockham who's won. And I think you can see why. Because it is very hard to understand things sometimes."

"So?"

"Well. I guess this is what I mean. Do I get emotional consolation from thinking about God? Sure. Does it mean I know all the answers? Well . . . no."

Silence.

"Thanks," I said after a while.

"The way I see it," he went on quickly and almost nervously, as if he had been wanting to say this for a long time, "there are, well, basically three views you can take about life. The first is that I don't understand it. The second is that I *can't* understand it. The third is that it doesn't make any sense."

"And which one do you take?"

"Usually the first. Sometimes the second."

"But never the third?"

He was silent.

"Hey, Tom," I said.

"Yes?"

"Is it light there yet?"

"Not yet."

"Well, tell me when it is, okay? I want to talk some more."

"I will."

The next day they came in with the dogs and helicopters.

We had waited so long to see them, but by that point I don't think any of us were in the mood. Instead we sat in the downstairs hallway. The boy Koizumi took out a deck of cards, and we played some three-card monte. Just to make things interesting, I put up a bank of two hundred dollars—money I'd been saving for drinks, drugs, I don't know what—and gave everyone twenty-five: me, the four kids, Tanaka, the detective, and one of his guys.

Tohru kept folding early. The cop broke even and the girl won about fifty, but it was the detective who really cleaned up. I think he was no stranger to the game, or maybe it was just that I couldn't read his poker face.

A Taiwanese cop apparently didn't think twice about gambling or taking bribes. Or coming out in the middle of a storm to look for missing girls. And I would be going back to New York City, where they fined you for spitting on the sidewalk.

The smokers were smoking. Koizumi tried a cigarette, but it just made him cough, and we laughed at him.

Then we would hear the roar of the helicopters right through the roof: *rum-rum-rum-rum. Rum-rum-rum.*

And men shouting and, though we might have imagined it, dogs barking.

They started looking at sunrise, just after seven. Then around eleven, just when we were starting to think about getting some lunch, one of the new cops came down and whispered in the detective's ear. He looked calm and excused himself, and his man went with him.

There was a suffocating silence. I could see Tanaka wanted to adjust his legs but couldn't. We looked at each other, hoping someone would speak.

Then the detective came back. He walked slowly, an old man's gait, his shoes turning out with each step. He settled back down heavily and lit a cigarette. We all looked at him but didn't say anything.

I noticed it was the "lucky" cigarette he'd turned upside down.

He smoked the entire thing. Then he dropped the butt in the paper cup from the tea he'd had with breakfast.

He looked up and said, "Mr. Taka?"

"Yes?"

"We've found your girls."

He'd addressed Tanaka, but I was the only one who responded.

"What?"

"I believe I was clear. We have found your girls."

No, I wanted to say. That wasn't possible. They couldn't be found.

They had disappeared in the interstices of the world, in the space between knowing the location of a particle and knowing its speed. They had disappeared into their own mystery. How could they be *found*—what did it even mean to say that?

But what I asked was, "Where? How?"

"Our men are very efficient."

In all my confusion I held back, and everyone held back, from asking the obvious question.

"Perhaps you had better accompany me," he said.

I got up, and Tanaka got up, and Tohru got up.

"I think that you had better stay here," the detective said to him.

Tohru shook his head.

I didn't say anything. I had tried reasoning with the kid before.

Boku wa iinchou. San nen kara kono kurasu no iinchou.

"Very well," said Chao.

Then Sumiregawa got up, too.

We all walked to the end of the hall and up the stairs into the sunlight. It was brilliant, like it had been the day before yesterday. The map room, with all its windows, was like a cathedral. We went out the front doors and into the heat and moisture.

Water stood in pools up to a foot deep. On the asphalt it had started to go up in delicate clouds of mist. Green leaves and fragments of branches were scattered around. The parking lot was full of cars and vans belonging to the Taiwanese Federal Police—it was a national park after all, federal territory—and men both in uniform and plainclothes, and three mongrel dogs in harnesses were resting under a tree. There was no sign of the helicopters. The men were standing around in uncertain attitudes; none of them were talking. I judged there might have been thirty of them.

On a yellow tarpaulin in the middle of the parking lot they had placed Pickett's body. He was lying faceup in the sun, and beside him—a little distance away—two girls also lay faceup.

It was like a dream or an illusion. And I had the sense, the distinct sense, that there had been a scene like this in my dreams the night before. I couldn't believe at all in its reality. But the heat and the bright sun were real enough, and I felt a splitting pain in my head.

The two girls lying faceup in pools of muddy water. Bloated and disfigured. Their hair like seaweed. Cuts on their bodies and faces. The details hit me one after another: familiar bowl-cut hair. The same uniform the girl Michiko was wearing. A yellow hair band. Some force was intent on stripping away any last possibility that these were two other girls, and all that was left was to imagine that I was dreaming.

I tried to grab Tohru's arm too late, and he ran across the asphalt and threw himself down over the body of the girl with the yellow hair band and lay there, heaving, for a while, then he lifted his head and screamed. None of the policemen stopped him. The screams rose and hung in the air, and I heard the screams of brothers whose sisters were dead, mothers whose children were dead.

The detective was standing next to me.

"Where did you find them?" I asked.

"A stone cistern, eight feet across and twenty feet deep. It was perhaps ten feet off the path. The mouth was covered by plants, but they broke the plants when they fell. The rains had floated the bodies to the surface. It stood in a clearing and was visible from the helicopter."

"And the girl in there?"

"Against all odds, she survived the fall and after several hours was able to climb out. One of the walls was slightly inclined."

Was that a miracle, or was it a miracle of another order that she had been in a hole?

"Cause of death?"

"We will see. But from my observations, one girl broke her neck, and the other most likely suffered a concussion and drowned."

"I see."

One of the policemen, pained by the sound of the screams that went on and on, made a move, but the detective caught his eye and shook his head.

I understood. The mystery was awful, but the truth was worse. It was better to scare ourselves with the mystery because the truth was that we were dead.

Back at the temple, when they had decided I was the Western intellectual type, they had reached into their drawer of skillful means and brought out some philosophical jazz about erasing the split between subject and object. And that had finally happened. The girls were dead, and so were we. Our lives had been hidden with them, and now they were brought out to lie there in the sun, and there was no kidding ourselves anymore.

Tohru got up and started to run. The policemen, under Chao's command, hesitated, and it was Sumiregawa who moved with quick steps and cut Tohru off, grappling him by the shoulders with impressive strength for such a slim boy. They stood there wrestling, Sumiregawa with a dead old man's face like the detective's. And we all watched as if it had nothing to do with us. The detective took out one more cigarette and lit it. Then he offered the pack to me and Tanaka. I took one, and Tanaka shook his head.

Tohru broke free and pushed Sumiregawa down on his back,

but he only made it a few steps before he collapsed himself, on his knees. Sumiregawa crawled to him and put his hand on his friend's knee.

The inarticulate screams had become a word as Tohru looked at Sumiregawa: *"Doushite? Doushite?"*

Why? Why?

Sumiregawa shook his head.

"Case closed?" I said to the detective.

Mouth clenched around his cigarette, Chao nodded.

I stuck out my hand.

"If I happen to write this up," I said, "I promise to make you look good."

"Thank you. Again I sympathize with your loss, and apologize for my suspicions."

Then he went forward. Two of the policemen had pulled Tohru up and were leading him back toward the building. That was the last I saw of Chao, with his back to me, saying loudly in Mandarin, "Identification is positive. Cover up the bodies. Call back the teams. The search is concluded."

And although he wasn't their commanding officer, the men said, "Yes, sir."

I was left with Tanaka. He made to bow but instead held out his hand to me.

"Mr. Neils, thank you for everything."

"Thanks for what?"

I'm sure he meant it. It was more than just a Japanese formality, but when it came to expressing his feelings, he couldn't find English words—or, perhaps, any.

To fill the pause I asked, "You'll go home?"

He nodded.

"I never asked. Where is home?"

"Morioka."

It wasn't any city I knew.

"I'm from Tono originally," he added, as if ashamed of having nothing to say.

"Oh, yeah? How is Tono?"

"Poor."

So that was that.

"You've got my card," I said.

"Hang on, give me another one and I'll write my number on the back."

So he did. I don't know if he'll ever drop me a line. If I were him, I suppose I wouldn't.

"Best of luck," I said.

"Thank you."

Inside. The girl Michiko cried and Koizumi patted her shoulder. Ms. Zhu looked sad and shook her head. The policemen all were quiet, but I was sure a part of them felt consoled because they had done their jobs.

Koizumi looked blank. "I just never thought this would happen."

"Me, neither."

"Nierusu-*san*," he said, "you know what we called you?"

What? I thought. Dirty old man? Crazy foreigner?"

"*Nii-san.*"

Big brother.

I gave him a hug.

"Kid, I'm really sorry. I guess it was all for nothing."

"No." He shook his head. "It wasn't for nothing."

But he couldn't say what he meant, either.

"*Nii-san,*" said Michiko in tears, and I hugged her, too.

"How's Class Rep?" Koizumi asked.

"About like you'd expect."

"Is he alright?"

"He will be. Your man Sumiregawa is looking out for him."

"I'd better go see him."

"Well, maybe you should give him some time."

"You know . . . he liked Kari a lot."

"I'm sure she was a wonderful girl."

"*Hontou nanda,*" he said. "She really was."

"I think I'd better get going. I'll hitch a ride with the cops. Nobody's going to want me around—you're going to have enough of the press, believe me. My advice is don't talk to anyone. You'll regret it later . . . when you see yourself up there."

He nodded.

"No," said Michiko, still holding on to me. "Don't go."

"I really think you guys need time to yourselves."

"Nierusu-*san,*" said Koizumi, "is there any way we can get in touch with you?"

So I gave him my card, too.

There was one more thing.

Before I turned it over to the police captain as part of the deceased's effects, I went through the contact list on Pickett's phone and found an entry marked *Mooooom*.

It was just after noon; I didn't know what time it would be where she was, but she picked up.

"Hello? Joshua?"

Her tone was harsh and demanding. She must have had caller ID.

"I'm sorry, Mrs. Pickett; I'm not your son."

"Who is this?"

Mrs. Pickett sounded like a crabby Southern lady who smoked too much. I got the feeling Josh hadn't really gotten along with her, and where that maybe should have made it better, I knew it made it much worse.

"Mrs. Pickett, my name is Peter Neils. I'm a journalist and . . . you know your son was a photographer."

"Of course I know all about the crazy things he does. What is this about?"

"Well, the thing is, Mrs. Pickett, maybe you knew your son was in Taiwan. . . ."

"Tai*wan*? Where is Tai*wan*?"

So she hadn't known.

"It's somewhere between Japan and China," I said. "Mrs. Pickett, your son and I were both in Taiwan on assignment. I was doing a story, and he was my cameraman, and . . ."

I kind of expected her to interrupt me again, but she didn't. I took a deep breath before I said, "Well, there was an accident, and I'm afraid I have to tell you. Well."

"What is it? What happened?"

"Josh passed away," I said. "Late yesterday evening."

I heard a stifled cry—a groan—that sounded more like anger than grief.

"Is this some kind of joke? Is this some kind of practical joke?"

"I'm very sorry, Mrs. Pickett, I wish I could tell you it isn't so. . . . You'll probably be hearing from the police, or the consulate, I don't know. But because I knew your son, I, well, I thought you might want to hear it from me first."

Crazy. Of course she didn't *want* to hear it at all.

There was a pause. Then she said thickly, slowly, "Oh, that stupid, stupid boy. That stupid boy."

"Josh was . . . a very good person, Mrs. Pickett, and . . . I was glad to know him."

"Christ," she whispered.

"He was doing what he loved."

Care to mention it was all your fault? I thought. You son of a bitch.

"Well, Mr. Neils . . . a mother has a right to know . . ."

"I'm sorry?"

"*How . . . ?*"

"Ah, yes—ah. Well. We had a terrible storm here. We were caught in it. And I, ah, I was going to fall off this . . . precipice at this gorge, where we are, and Josh tried to catch me. And his foot slipped."

Of course I should have been prepared for the question. As it happened, I answered without thinking. Although for all the elaborateness of the lie, I could have managed to phrase it a little better.

There was a thick silence for a minute. Then Mrs. Pickett's

voice, like an old radio coming back into focus, resumed, "Mr. Neils, you sound like a terribly nice person."

"Maybe I'll look you up when I'm back in the States," I said. "I just wanted to tell you."

But she had already hung up.

TOHRU MARUYAMA

We **were** back in Taipei. The air was nasty, smoggy; but out on the hotel balcony, with the stars right overhead, you felt like you were closer to heaven and it didn't bother you.

I was standing there, looking out at the city, holding Kari's hair band in one hand. I know. I *know*—but what was I supposed to do? There were so many lights. So many people. They didn't know us, and they didn't care if we were alive or dead.

We'd gotten back to the hotel the night before, and the next day we'd be on a plane back to Japan. The night before— lying there in the new room they'd given me with Koizumi and Sumiregawa, figuring we'd want to be together, not thinking I'd ever get to sleep but then waking up six hours later—I'd had a dream.

I was in the empty classroom where just a year ago I'd been cleaning up with Kari and she had done *okiyome* on my soul, and it was just like then, still and quiet and beautiful. Kari was sitting there—it didn't surprise me; I didn't know in the dream that she was gone—reading a story to a bunch of little kids, like toddlers. She was always so good with kids. At first they kept messing around, but she didn't lose her patience. Then one by one they started listening. I couldn't hear the story, but I was listening, too, like I was one of those kids.

But there was one kid who just couldn't sit still. No matter how many times Kari looked at him with her gentle eyes, he kept trying to crawl away. So I said to him (I couldn't tell if I said it out loud), Hey, if you think you can tell a better story, go right ahead!

Then I woke up. It was six in the morning, my head hurt, and I was sick of being alive.

I don't know if the dream was good or bad. If it was about something in the future, I didn't think there was any future.

Sumiregawa came out on the balcony in his undershirt, a cigarette in one hand and his lighter in the other. He saw me. I didn't say anything, but like out of consideration for me, he didn't light up right away.

"Sorry," he said, sounding less smart and more normal than ever. "Did you want to be alone?"

I shrugged.

"Or . . . if you want to talk or anything."

But that was just the thing; I didn't want to talk. Then, like he was reading my mind, he said, "I get it. I don't want to talk, either."

All the kids—the girls especially—had tried to talk to me: Otsuki Sakura, Chizu Sato, Mari Ogami, and Jin-*kun*. But I had nothing to say. I tried to be polite, but I was just going through the motions—doing what was expected of me.

"You know, I was thinking," said Sumiregawa, playing with his cigarette.

"When *aren't* you thinking?"

"Ha. But no. It's something I read once—that when the soldiers came back from the war, a lot of them had trouble talking about it. I mean, you'd think they couldn't *stop* talking about it—they'd had this *experience*, and even if no one else could imagine it, you'd think they'd keep trying to explain."

"We weren't in a war," I said quietly.

"Maybe not. But it's just, those are the kind of experiences we have now."

Then Koizumi came out. He'd been sweating and the sleeves of his coat were rolled up.

"Hey, guys."

"How's Kamakiri?" I said.

"Good." He swallowed. "I think. She's asleep. She's been through a lot. I mean, we *all* have, but like—"

"No, I get you."

I kept working Kari's hair band through my hands, like prayer beads.

"Hey, Seiji-*kun*," I said. "I'm sorry I pushed you down."

"It's okay."

"I mean, you probably saved my life."

For what it's worth.

He lit his cigarette. The smoke started to drift out toward the lights of the city.

"I was thinking, too," I said. "I'm going to join Mahikari."

I didn't know until I said it that I *was* thinking that. But what else could I do? Maybe that was what the dream meant: that it was my turn, now, to start telling the story. That was the only way it made sense.

I bet that's what she would say if she were here. I knew where the center was in Morioka and everything. She was always trying to get people to join, and people went sometimes, just to be polite. But I would go, and I would do whatever they told me.

"Really?" was all Koizumi said, and Sumiregawa didn't say anything.

I looked at Koizumi, but he looked away.

"I guess I was thinking, too."

"Oh, yeah?"

"I was just thinking . . . when all we played Egyptian Rat-screw." He grinned. It looked like it took a lot out of him. "That was a lot of fun . . . right?"

"Sure."

"I mean, we were just playing a game. But I kind of feel like that was the coolest thing we ever did."

"Yeah," I said, nodding. "Maybe it was."

HSIEN CHAO

It truly was a pleasant day, as often when a typhoon blows over. On the road to Taipei, the pavement was like crushed black jewels, and a light haze hung on the sea. I'd seen the view from that cliff-hugging road far too many times to consider it beautiful—but like a man's wife, there are times, even after many years, when something like that can surprise you.

The cars crawled down the road one after another. Obediently we came; obediently we went. The radio was silent.

Sheng sat in the passenger seat playing with his buttons. For the past half hour he'd looked like he wanted to say something, or like he expected me to say something. But he should have known me better than that.

I looked at his nervous face, his woman's eyebrows. I knew something was going on in there, but it was as distant from me as my hometown.

Why do men bother growing up? Only to let their children make the same mistakes. The old people always write books, and the young people read them and get it all wrongheaded. Each generation thinking no one before it has suffered when the bookstores, the libraries, the writing on tombstones are about nothing else.

All at once a plume of smoke on our right caught my eye—but I should have known the road by now. It wasn't arson, it was that big Daoist temple, Eternal Light Crystal or whatever it was. How many times had I driven past without even slowing down? On holidays, which they were always having for the anniversary of some god's marriage to the fisherman's daughter, the place was vomiting cars.

Tapping the wheel, I thought. Then I flicked on the radio and spoke: "Captain Zhao, you read? I'm going to make a pit stop."

"Detective? Don't tell me you're out of tobacco already."

"I'd like to start a fresh pack. It's good luck."

His laugh came through hoarse and crackly. "You are the most superstitious man I ever met."

I bristled a little, especially knowing Sheng heard. Surely that wasn't true.

"Go to hell. Anyhow I'll catch you up, I know the route."

Without waiting for his reply I signed off, then pulled abruptly to the shoulder of the road. Sheng had been in a daze; he looked up and blinked.

"Uncle?"

"Didn't you hear me?" I said as I climbed out. "I want more cigarettes. But first we're going in here."

"Here . . . ?"

His eyes took in the huge roof of the temple's outer sanctuary, sloped and peaked as if it were sagging under its load of pastel dragons and other nonsense. Sheng followed me with his head down, knowing better than to ask questions.

After the typhoon there weren't many worshippers, only a few old men smoking cigarettes in the parking lot. The entire temple stood in clouds of smoke, both from the worshippers—by some foolish law you couldn't smoke in Buddhist temples, but the old gods seemed to have no problem with it—and from their ritual fires and incense pits.

It was very quiet. I could hear my left boot squeaking from where I'd worn it smooth on those cursed trails.

We walked together into the reek of incense, under the eaves dripping faded gold, the chewed-up cement underfoot, aged not by time but by the masses and masses of people who came here daily to throw their prayers at the gods. They must have tired the gods out, made them old. The place looked and felt like it had been standing for hundreds of years.

I reached the desk, where a young girl stood, her eyes watering from the smoke, bored and unpretty. On either side of her mounds of talismans, fortunes, and charms, each price marked nicely in black pen. Long life, only five hundred Taiwan dollars. I suppose you would live longer than if you spent the money on cigarettes.

"Give me this much joss."

I put down my money, and she handed across the bundle of spells on worthless pulp-paper, almost as big as the phone book. For pocket change, a man could be a spiritual millionaire. Then she forgot about us, although we were standing right there, and went back to staring into space.

"Uncle," Sheng whispered to me, his curiosity finally starting to get the better of him, "what are we doing?"

"What does it look like we're doing? We're making sacrifices for the dead."

He shuffled his feet.

"I thought my sister raised you properly. Haven't you got any respect?"

"But Uncle . . ."

"But what?"

"You always say it doesn't do any good."

"Be quiet and carry these."

We threw them, a few handfuls each, into the door of the furnace where yesterday's offerings were still hissing mounds of coal.

Sheng glanced at me sideways, then lowered his head and shut his eyes.

I cuffed him. "Not here, boy. Pray over there."

I pointed to the sanctuary, up the stairs and under another folded double roof where the gods of the temple sat in darkness, feeding off toxic fumes. We passed an old lady going down, still muttering some prayer under her breath. I almost offered her my arm, until I remembered I was nearly as old as she was.

We came up and stood in front of the door to the other world. With the sun overhead and the lanterns out, there was no seeing inside except for a fleck here and there of gold, itself stained half black by the smoke. In front of us the incense sticks, like parodies of human lives, burned slowly down in a trough of dirty sand.

"Hell," I said, slapping my pockets, "we forgot incense."

"I'm sorry!" yelped Sheng.

"Be quiet; it isn't your fault."

After all, it had been a while.

I took a Peony cigarette out of the nearly empty pack and stuck it, filter down, in the incense trough, then lit it. In the trickle of smoke I put my hands together. I looked into that darkness, and for a moment it looked as if the smoke were rushing out of it, or being sucked into it.

I felt something. But what it was, I didn't care to think about.

Every day thousands of prayers were poured inside, for the living and dead, recovery from illness, recovery of lost things, patience, wisdom, courage. Millions of prayers if you counted everyone across the world. And where did they go? They must go somewhere. Nothing in this world really disappears.

After a moment I heard muttering—faintly, as if from miles away. Were those the prayers, rebounding back on us? Or were they the voices of the lost, answering us when we called to them? But I looked up and it was only Sheng, his head bowed and his eyes shut, hands clasped together, flapping his gums.

I cuffed his head, and he started, pulled back from whatever cloud he had floated up to.

"What? What?"

"Don't act like a fool," I said. "Just shut your mouth and pray."

ACKNOWLEDGMENTS

Big thanks are due to Fred Ramey at Unbridled Books; my agent, Eve Bridburg, the Virgil without whom I could never have navigated the publishing world; and again to Chris Castellani. I understand it's the conventional wisdom that writers rarely help other writers get published, but Chris apparently doesn't hold with conventional wisdom.

Thanks of a different order to Professor T. Griffith Foulk, the only convincing Buddhist I've ever met; to my fellow students in the Woodenfish program; and to the kind folks of the Fo Guang Shan (Buddha's Light Mountain) organization—especially Venerable Huifeng and Jason Clower—for hosting us and teaching us about Chinese Buddhism—but I'm still not converting. Nice try.

To other academics without whom I ~~might not~~ would not have survived college: Edward Allen Baker, Amlin Gray, Phil Swoboda, Brian Morton, Danny Kaiser, and last but certainly not least Sayuri Oyama—*itsumo gomeiwaku sumimasen deshita.*

Finally, heartfelt thanks to three people who had nothing to do with the creation of this book: Takeru, Kazuyo, and Nanane

Ogawa, the greatest host family in all of Saitama prefecture, possibly in all of Japan. You guys may never know how much those months we spent together meant to me; hell, I couldn't even explain to you why I couldn't bring myself to kill that cockroach. *Mata isshou ni taiyaki tabeyouyo—itsuka.*